HOT as puck

A Bad Motherpuckers Novel

By Lili Valente

HOT
as puck

By Lili Valente

Self Taught Ninja Press

About the Book

The NHL's biggest bad boy is about to fall for the virgin next door...

I am the world's biggest dating failure. We're talking my last date went home with our waitress kind of failure.

But I have an ace in the back pocket of my mom jeans—my sexy-as-sin best friend, NHL superstar forward, Justin Cruise.

Justin owes me favors dating back to seventh grade, long before he became a hotshot with a world famous…stick. So in return for my undying platonic loyalty, all I want is an easy-peasy crash course on how to be a sex goddess.

How hard can it be?

***

I have never been so hard in my life.

The things I want to do to my sweet, kindergarten-teaching, mitten-crocheting best friend Libby Collins are ten different kinds of wrong. Maybe twenty.

But I'm a firm believer in teaching by example, and by the end of our first lesson, we've graduated to a *hands on* approach to her sexual education: my hands all over her, her hands all over me, and her hot mouth melting beneath mine as I prove to her there isn't a damned thing wrong with the way she kisses.

Give me a month, and I'll transform Libby from wall flower to wall banger, and ensure she's confident enough to seduce any guy she wants.

Problem is… the only guy I want her seducing is me.

Hot as Puck is a sexy, flirty, friends-to-lovers Standalone romantic comedy from *USA Today* Bestseller Lili Valente.

Dedicated to Sylvia Pierce, a talented author and gifted friend.

CHAPTER
One

Justin

This is it, the night I'll look back on in fifty or sixty years and stab a finger at as the moment my life changed forever. Somewhere out there, in the throng of people wiggling to the club beat pulsing across the Portland skyline from the most exclusive rooftop lounge in the city, is the woman I'm going to marry.

Next summer.

In eight short months.

Because I'm dying to settle down, develop a food-baby where my six-pack used to be, spend Friday nights on the couch in my give-up-on-life sweatpants arguing about what to watch on Netflix and picking out names for the five or six kids my wife and I will bang out as quickly as possible to ensure we'll have an army of small people to share in the grinding monotony of our wedded bliss.

Ha. Right.

Or rather *no*. Hell no. Fuck no, with a side of "what kind of reality-altering drugs have you been huffing in the bathroom?"

Sylvia is out of her goddamned mind! I'm twenty-eight years old—tonight, happy fucking birthday to me—and at the top of my game. I have zero interest in a long-term commitment to anything but my team.

The Portland Badgers are riding a ten-game winning streak, thanks largely to the fact that I bust my ass in the gym every other morning so I can bust my ass on the ice every time Nowicki spaces-out eighteen minutes into the period and forgets what his stick is for. That rookie's untreated ADHD is a pain in my ass, but the rest of the forwards and I are taking up the slack and then some. I'm averaging over a point a game, leading the league in goals, and on my way to an elite season. Maybe even an Art Ross Trophy-winning season, though I don't like to count my eggs before they've been scrambled, smothered in cheese and hot sauce, and wrapped in a burrito.

God, a burrito sounds good. I'm so fucking hungry. I would kill for Mexican right now, or at least something cooked and wrapped in something other than seaweed.

Nearly three thousand dollars in hor d'oeuvres are being passed around this party on shiny silver platters, and there's not a damned thing I want to eat.

I let Sylvia—who has very firm opinions about many, many things—handle ordering the food, and apparently she thought sushi, sushi, more sushi, and some weird, rock-hard, low-fat cookies that taste like vanilla-flavored air were all anyone would want to shove in their pie-hole tonight. Just like she thought I should get down on one knee and put a ring on her finger in time to plan a blockbuster summer wedding or she would need to "explore her other options."

Explore her other fucking options. What the fuck? Who says something like that to a guy they swear they're desperately in love with? If she were really that gone on me, wouldn't I be the *only* option? The only person in the entire world that she could even remotely consider spending the rest of her life with?

I kind of want to hate Sylvia—what sort of person tries to blackmail you into proposing to them on *your* birthday? She should have at least waited until *her* birthday next month—but I just keep thinking about how lonely my bed is going to be tonight. Sylvia is clearly deeply deluded about how far along we are in the evolution of our relationship, but she's also very pretty, gives the best head I've ever had, bar none, and smells really, really nice.

I have a thing about the way a woman smells. Not her perfume or her soap or her body lotion, but *her*. The woman herself. Her base note, the scent that rises from her skin when she's lying in the sun or kissing me after a run or just hasn't showered in a while.

Yes, with the right woman, I enjoy logging some quality bedroom time while she's a little bit dirty. Don't fucking judge me! It's my birthday!

Anyway… No one smells as good as Sylvia does at the end of a long day on my boat, with sweat, sea salt, and sunscreen dried on her skin. Making love to her on the deck this past summer, with her long legs wrapped around my waist as I did my best to take home the trophy for most orgasms delivered in a single afternoon, I was convinced I'd finally met someone I could stick with for longer than a season.

But it's not going to happen. It's only October and I've just told Sylvia she's coo-coo for Cocoa Puffs and that I'll have her shit packed up and sent to her office tomorrow afternoon.

And then she said that I was an emotionally unavailable jerk who is incapable of sustaining an adult relationship. And then I said that she's a blackmailing, birthday-ruining, manipulative, sushi-obsessed control freak who should try to choke down a carb once in a while because it might make her more fun to be around on pizza night or donut morning or any other day of the goddamned week involving carbs because a life without carbs is a stupid life. And then she flipped me off and told me to "have a nice long, lonely existence, asshole," before knocking over a tray of champagne glasses on her way to the elevator at the other end of the roof.

The only good news? Very few of my guests seemed to notice our fight or Sylvia's dramatic exit.

It's nine-thirty, we've all been drinking since six, and most of my nearest and dearest are feeling no pain. I should be feeling no pain, too. I'm on my third tumbler of GlenDronach, haven't eaten anything since lunch because the food at my party is unacceptable—if Sylvia and I were really meant to be, she would have realized I hated sushi two months ago—and haven't drunk anything more serious than a beer since before the preseason.

But somehow, I'm stone-cold sober.

Sober and tired of celebrating, and wishing I could slip out and grab a deep-dish pizza from Dove Vivi. The cornmeal crust thing they've done to their pies is addictive, and I'm pretty sure there's nothing in the world fresh mozzarella, house-made bacon, and a hearty slathering of pesto can't fix.

Portland is home to some of the best eats in the world. It's also home to more strip clubs per capita than any other city in the nation. If I weren't committed to being a good host, I could have pizza in my belly and boobs in my face in under an hour. But I'm not the kind to ghost on my guests. I leave that for weirdos like my team captain, Brendan, who consistently vanishes from bars and clubs without warning, and clearly has issues with saying good-bye.

Not that I can blame him. After six years as a happily married man, going back to hitting the scene solo can't be easy.

I'm just glad to see him finally out and about again. After Maryanne's death, he shut down so hard a lot of us on the team were worried there might come a day when we'd show up for practice and learn Brendan wasn't coming back to the ice, either because he'd lost the will to play, or because he'd lost the will to live.

That's how much you should love the woman you're going to marry. You should love her so much that if she were taken away from you it would feel like your rib cage had been cracked open and some sadistic son of a bitch was cutting away tiny pieces of your heart, slathering them in salt, and eating them right in front of you.

I've never felt anything close to that. For Sylvia or any other girl I've dated.

So maybe Sylvia is right. Maybe I'm going to spend the rest of my life solo, with my loneliness occasionally broken by short-term relationships with various hot pieces of ass.

"Poor me," I say, lips curving in a hard grin.

Seriously, cry me a river, right? I've got a multi-million-dollar contract, a stunning loft with one-hundred and eighty degree views of the city, and my health, which is not something I'm stupid enough to take for granted. I was born with the kind of face that not even a black eye from scrumming with those douchebags from L.A. can wreck, and a body that performs—on the ice and in the bedroom. I should be laughing all the way to the dance floor, where I know of at least six or seven unattached hotties, any one of which would be happy to ease my birthday breakup pain by riding my cock all night long.

What do I want instead?

Pizza. My pajamas. And a crochet hook with an endless supply of yarn.

Nothing calms me down like hooking on a granny square until I've got one big enough to cover my entire damned bed. I've graduated to more complex projects since those early days learning how to hook so I wouldn't go crazy while I was stuck in bed with mono for three months, but sometimes mindless repetition is the only cure for what ails me.

And yes, I like to crochet. Again, I'll ask that you not fucking judge me, because it's my birthday, because my charity, Hookers for the Homeless, has provided over two thousand caps, gloves, and scarves to people in need, and because my Instagram account—Hockey Hooker—has over a million followers. Clearly, the women of the world have no problem with a man who enjoys handicrafts. Though, the fact that my first post was a body shot of me wearing nothing but a Santa Hat I'd crocheted over my cock probably didn't hurt.

I have no shame when it comes to selfies with my latest project. My friend Laura—childhood partner in crime and current public relations master for the Badgers—says she approves of my social media efforts to promote good will for the team. Her little sister and my crochet guru, Libby, thinks it's great that I'm using my yarn addiction to raise awareness of the homeless crisis. But let's get real. I started posing semi-nude for the tail and the attention.

I'm usually a big fan of tail and attention.

But now, as Laura and Libby climb the steps leading up to the patio from the dance floor, clearly intending to wish me a warm, bubbly, old-friends happy birthday, I wish I had an excuse not to talk to either one of them. Laura because she's insane when she's drunk—once she's had a few, the usually level-headed La can't be trusted not to embarrass herself and everyone around her—and Libs because I'm incapable of hiding anything from that girl.

Ever since thirteen-year-old Libs spent months teaching me how to crochet when I was housebound my sophomore year of high school—keeping me company and furthering my yarn-based education while we watched 80s movies and debated important things like whether *Better Off Dead* or *Just One of the Guys* was the superior underrated teen flick of that particular decade—I've had a chink in my armor where the youngest Collins sibling is concerned.

She sees through me. Every damned time.

When I had a shitty first half of my first season with the Badgers five years ago, Libby was the one who noticed I was being eaten alive by self-doubt and talked me back from the edge. When my charity was getting audited by the IRS, Libby realized I wasn't nearly as chill about the whole thing as I was pretending to be and sent me a knight's helmet she'd crocheted and a note promising that everything would work out. And when Sylvia and I had a pregnancy scare last summer, Libby was the only person I told.

Hearing Libs say that I could absolutely handle being a dad had made me a little less terrified. Not that I'd believed her, but hearing that trying your best and loving your kid is all that really matters from a woman who spends every day with a classroom full of rug-rats was comforting.

But I don't want to be comforted right now. I want to get through the rest of this party and then hide out at home and lick my breakup wounds in private. So I plaster on a smile and hope it's too dark for Libby to see how shitty I feel.

"Hello, birthday boy!" Laura throws her long arms around me, hugging me hard enough to make my breath rush out with an *oof* as she crushes my ribs, reminding me she's also freakishly strong when she's three sheets to the wind. "I love you, Justin. I'm so glad we're still best friends. Let's go do happy-birthday shots on the roof to celebrate!"

"We're already on the roof." I grunt again as she hugs me even tighter.

"Yes, we are, and as high up as anyone needs to be right now," Libby agrees, meeting my pained gaze over her sister's shoulder, her brown eyes anxious. Clearly, she's also aware that her big sis has entered the bad-decision-making portion of the evening and should be monitored closely until she's home in bed.

"No, the real roof, the one through the locked door behind the DJ booth." Laura points a wobbly hand toward the stairwell on the other side of the dance floor, then twists her long red hair into a knot on top of her head. "I've been practicing my lock-picking skills so I'll be ready when I quit PR to become a spy."

"As one does," I observe dryly.

"Exactly!" Laura jabs a bony finger into the center of my chest. "See, you get it. So let's do this. We'll break the lock, climb the stairs, and be the highest things in downtown. Get shots and meet me there. Or maybe we should stick with martinis." She moans happily as she wiggles her fingers in the general direction of the bar. "Those Thai basil martinis are so amazing! Perfect with the sushi. Like, seriously brilliant. Sylvia did a bang-up job with the catering, Jus. Especially for a woman who looks like she hasn't eaten since last Christmas."

"Laura, hush," Libby whispers, nudging her

sister in the ribs with her elbow.

Laura bares her teeth in an "oh shit" grimace before smacking herself on the forehead. "Fuck, I'm sorry. I forgot about the storming out and knocking over a tray of drinks on her way out of the party thing. Are you two okay?"

"We're fine," I say, cursing silently. So much for avoiding this particular conversation. "She just decided it wasn't working for her. It's no big deal."

"But breaking up on your birthday sucks." Laura's lips turn down hard at the edges. "And I thought she was one of the nice ones. I mean, I didn't know her that well, but she seemed nice."

"She was nice." I take another too big drink of my scotch. "And now she's gone. But she hadn't even unpacked her boxes yet, so it shouldn't take long to move them all out."

"That's right. I forgot you two had moved in together. Bet that makes you want to keep drinking, huh?" Laura reaches back, putting an arm around Libby, hugging her much shorter sister closer as she not-so-subtly tries to steal Libby's martini.

Libby, who I suddenly realize is looking very un-Libby-like in a tight black tank top and a pair of leather pants that cling to her curvy thighs, huffs and swats Laura's hand away. "Enough! Stop using displays of affection to try to steal my drink."

"Why? It worked last time," Laura says,

grinning wickedly.

"Well, it's not going to work this time. I'm keeping my martini." Libby narrows her eyes, which are ringed in heavy black liner and some silver glittery stuff that emphasizes how enormous they are. It's a look that's way more rock-star than kindergarten teacher and also decidedly…odd. For her, anyway.

I can't remember the last time I saw Libby wearing makeup or tight clothing. She's a "layers of linen draped around her until she looks like an adorable bag lady or a hippie pirate" kind of girl. I'm used to the Libby who wears ruffly dresses, clogs, and crocheted sweaters, and totes her knitting bag with her everywhere she goes.

This new look is so unexpected that I'm distracted long enough for Laura to snatch my scotch right out of my hand.

"Hey, give that back," I say, scowling as she dances out of reach. "It's an open bar, psycho. Go get your own scotch."

"But it's more fun to steal yours," Laura says. And then, with the gleeful giggle of a woman who is going to be very hungover tomorrow morning, she turns and flees into the throng of dancers writhing to the music, tossing, "Come get me when it's time to break and enter! You know you want to," over her shoulder.

Libby sighs heavily, and I turn back to see her watching me with that same anxious expression, making my heart lurch. "I don't want to talk about Sylvia," I say, cutting her off before she can ask.

"Okay," she says, letting me off the hook far more easily than I expect her to. "But can we talk about something else? Something kind of…private?"

"Um, sure." I do a quick scan of our immediate surroundings. Aside from a couple making out in the shadows about ten feet away, we're alone. Everyone else is either out on the dance floor, queued up at the bar, or lounging on the couches near the fire pit on the other side of the patio, soaking in the view of the city.

"Thanks." Libby smiles nervously as she lifts her glass. "Just let me down a little more liquid courage first."

"All right," I say, wondering who this woman is and what she's done with my sweet, rarely drinks more than one drink, doesn't own a stitch of black clothing, would never leave the house without putting on a bra Libby.

I really don't think she's wearing a bra under that lacy shirt. And I really can't stop staring, trying to solve the bra or no-bra mystery, and I'm swiftly becoming way too fixated on Libby's breasts for my personal comfort.

"Maybe I should get a drink, too." I start for the bar, needing a moment to pull myself together, when Libby puts a hand on my arm.

"I'm sorry," she says, but I have no idea what she's apologizing for, only that her touch feels different than it did before. As different as the Libby I've known since she was a kid is from this seriously sexy woman standing in front of me.

CHAPTER
Two

Justin

Libby pulls her hand away, fiddling with the stem of her martini glass, and the flash of heat her touch inspired vanishes. I shake my head, certain I must have imagined it. I've known Libby forever. She's like a little sister to me. It's probably just the alcohol on an empty stomach catching up with me.

"I tried to keep Laura from ordering a third martini," Libby continues, cluing me in as to why she's sorry. "But she swore her tolerance was better than it used to be."

I arch a brow. "And you believed her?"

"Good point." She laughs. "Though to be fair, you should have known better than to invite her to a party with an open bar."

"I did," I say with a grin. "But I did it anyway. Neither of us can be trusted to make good decisions. You know that. It's one of the reasons we're friends."

"Partners in crime is more like it." Libby shakes her head as she brushes her glossy brown hair over her shoulder, bringing my attention back to that wicked little tank top.

Jesus, it's tight.

I force my gaze back to her face—the only part of Libby that I should be staring at—as she says, "Promise me you won't let her up on the real roof, okay? There probably aren't any guardrails up there, and she needs enclosed spaces right now."

"I promise." I lean against the wall behind me as I do another quick scan of rocker Libby. "So, what's with the new look, Libs? Did you get attacked on the street by one of those makeover shows?"

"No, I wasn't attacked on the street." She rolls her eyes, shrugging as she takes a sip of her martini. "I just thought it was time to try something new."

"Well, that's certainly new."

Her brow furrows. "I take that to mean you don't like it?"

"No, I like it. I mean…" I trail off, unsure what to say. On any other woman, I probably *would* like the outfit—what's not to like about boobs out for show and tell? But this is Libby. "It's just different."

"So? What's wrong with putting myself out

there a little on a Friday night?"

"Or a lot out there," I tease.

"Fine. Or a lot." She stands up straighter, rolling her shoulders back, making certain shapely, lovely things even harder to ignore. "I may choose to wear modest clothing most of the time, Justin, but I'm perfectly aware of the power of showing a little skin. I've had boobs since the fifth grade, you know."

I blink. Hard. "Are you drunk, too?"

"No, I'm not drunk." She sets her drink down on the bar table beside me with a huff. "Though I'm starting to wish I were. Are you trying to make me feel ridiculous and insecure?"

"No!" I lift my hands in surrender. "Sorry, I've just never heard you say the word boobs before. Let alone…" I start to motion toward her breasts, but think better of it and play it off by running a hand through my hair. "Yeah. You just caught me off guard."

"But I'm right, aren't I?" She steps closer, holding my gaze.

I frown. "Right about what?"

"Be honest." Her voice goes soft as she lifts one nearly bare shoulder. "You're having to work hard not to look at my chest right now, aren't you?"

"No," I lie, even as my traitorous eyeballs flick down for another quick glimpse of the creamy swells rising above the black lace of her shirt.

"Ha! See there!" she crows, pointing a

triumphant finger at my rapidly heating face. "See! I knew it! I knew you were trying not to look!"

"It was the power of suggestion," I say defensively, wishing I still had my scotch. I could really use something to hide my lying mouth behind. "It's like when someone tells you not to look directly at the sun. As soon as the words are out, you can't help looking right at it."

"No, *you* can't help looking right at it. Most people have the common sense not to do things that are going to damage their retinas."

"Are you saying I have no common sense?"

"Are you saying my breasts are like the sun?" she counters, stepping so close I can feel the heat of her body and smell her Libby smell rising in the air around me.

I take a deeper breath, realizing for the first time that Libby smells *good*. Not simply good as in clean and inoffensive to the nostrils, but good as in I would like to know what she smells like after she hasn't showered in a while. I would like to smell the curve of her neck after she's fresh off a run, to pull her sports bra up and over her head and let my tongue explore the sweat-damp valley between those incredible, way-more-than-a-handful—

"I need a drink." I cut the thought off before it—or the erection swelling behind the zipper of my jeans—can fully form. I refuse to think those kinds of thoughts about Libby. It's so wrong that wrong isn't a strong enough word for it.

I'm trying to think of a better word, something appropriate for things forbidden, disturbing, and a little embarrassing, when Libby puts a hand on my arm again, curling her fingers into the cotton of my dress shirt.

"Can we talk about the private stuff first?" Uncertainty creeps back into her gaze. "I'm afraid if I wait, I'll lose my nerve and never say what I came over here to say."

I swallow hard, fighting the urge to bolt. "What did you come over to say?"

"I have a favor to ask." Her teeth worry her bottom lip in a way that makes the newly aware of Libby part of me wonder what her mouth tastes like.

Fuck. I have to get away from her and get my head on straight before I do something stupid like try to kiss her and ruin one of the best friendships I've ever had.

I've never even *thought* about dating either of the Collins sisters, no matter how nice they are to look at. They are my friends, so close we're almost family. I'm the guy who glares at their boyfriends at the annual holiday party our parents throw together and who makes veiled threats about pounding faces if those douches even *think* about hurting Libby or La. I'm the big-brother type, not the guy trying to scam his way into Libby's pants. Or down her shirt. Or daydreaming about slipping my tongue between her lips while I cup her breasts in my hands and—

"A kind of strange favor," Libby continues, derailing the smut train in my mind just in time. *Thank God.* "But the fact that you and Sylvia broke up makes it a little less strange, I guess." She laughs nervously. "I mean, not that I was ever going to ask you to do something that would get you in trouble with your girlfriend. I'm desperate, but I'm not crazy. Well, maybe a little crazy, but—"

"Just spit it out, Libs." Sweat breaks out beneath my shirt as I fight not to think about lips or breasts or giving Libby anything but a firm, friendly hug.

"Okay, fine." She pulls in a breath and lets it out in a rush. "I need you to teach me about sex."

My eyebrows shoot up and I'm pretty sure I would have spit out my drink if Laura hadn't stolen it. "What?" I sputter, even though I heard her perfectly well. But hearing and believing are two entirely different things.

"Sex," she repeats, her cheeks going pink. "And flirting and being sexy and not saying stupid things on the first date or the second date or the third date. All that kind of stuff. The stuff I'm clearly really bad at."

"Um, I—" I break off with a choked sound. "I'm sorry, Libs, but—"

"I'm going to be twenty-five in three months, Jus," she cuts in, a pleading note in her voice.

"And I'm still shy and weird and completely hopeless with men. If something doesn't change, I'm going to spend the rest of my life alone, crocheting bonnets for my cats and wondering what it's like to have a real relationship."

"You don't even have cats," I say, because I don't know what to say to the rest of it. I know Libby doesn't date much, but I had no idea she was so upset about it.

"I will by then. I'll have so many cats I'll barely be able to walk from my couch to the bathroom without stepping on one. And when I die of old age, the poor things will run out of cat food and end up eating my corpse."

"Well, there are worse ways to go," I joke. "I hope to go of old age myself, and once you're dead you probably won't mind—"

"Justin, please!" Her brow furrows and desperation creeps into her eyes. "Please be serious. I'm being serious. I need help and you're the only person I can ask."

"What about Laura?" I shove my hands into my pockets, wishing I'd run for it while I still had the chance. Before things got well and truly weird. "She's good at flirting. I'm not sure about sex, because she's my friend and thinking about her having sex is almost as gross as thinking about *you* having sex, but I'm—"

"Thanks a lot," Libby interrupts, her bottom lip trembling as she reclaims her drink with a swift snatching motion that sends the liquid sloshing out of the glass. "It's nice to know the thought of me in an intimate relationship with someone is *that* repulsive."

"I didn't mean it that way, Libs. I just meant—"

"It doesn't matter." She downs the rest of her martini in one gulp before setting it back on the table with a hard *clink*. "I never should have asked you for help. This was a mistake."

"Come on, Libs, I didn't mean to hurt your feelings." I reach for her, but she steps away, lifting a hand between us.

"Don't. I can't deal with a pity hug right now." Her lips press together as she blinks hard. "Let's just pretend this never happened, okay? I'll find someone else to help me. Or I won't. It doesn't really matter, right? I mean, what's another spinster kindergarten teacher eaten by cats?"

"Libby, wait," I call after her as she turns and walks away, tottering in her too-high-and-stabby-looking-for-Libby-to-be-wearing heels.

But she doesn't turn back, and now I feel even more like shit than I did before. Watching Libby storm away from me is much, much harder than watching Sylvia do the same. So hard, in fact, that I can't let it happen. I follow her, weaving my way through the crowd. But when I get to the other side of the dance floor, she's nowhere to be found.

And damn it, I feel like something's been lost. Something necessary and special that maybe I've taken for granted.

Right then, I make a promise to myself to find Libby and do my best to help her out, no matter how uncomfortable it might be at first. Friends don't let friends get eaten by cats, and Libby's been my friend for too long for me to say no when she needs me to say yes.

CHAPTER
Three

Libby

Stupid, stupid, stupid! How could you be so stupid? Seriously, what were you thinking, stupid? Did you honestly think you would be able to pull this off? What is wrong *with you?!*

Loneliness is what's wrong with me. I'm lonely and so desperate for a change that I'm willing to do things I've never done before. But asking Justin for help was clearly *not* the solution to my problem. All I've done is freak him out on his birthday and force him to confess that he is among one of the many, many men in the world who find it distasteful to imagine me in bed without my clothes on.

God, I'm never going to live that down. *Never.*

I'm so embarrassed I can't lift my gaze from the floor. I push through the crowd with my chin tucked to my chest, hurry around the edge of the dance floor as fast as my insanely-high heels will allow, and swing through the glass door leading out of the private party and into Bobo's public bar, trying not to hyperventilate with shame. But my cheeks are hot, tears are rising in my eyes, and my ribs are doing their best to squeeze my heart into a puddle of misery juice. All I want to do is run home, dive under the covers, and hide there for the rest of the weekend.

But I can't leave. Laura is still out there, living it up, and I have to stay and make sure my sister doesn't get on the wrong train home, the way she did on the Fourth of July, the last time she had more than two drinks. I may be terrible at flirting, partying, dancing, or doing anything else remotely cool, but I'm a good sister.

"A damned good sister," I grumble as I slide onto a stool at the end of the bar. "You're going to owe me for this one, La. Big time."

I order a glass of white wine—happy to pay for a drink as long as it means I can hide out here in the near darkness of the ultra-modern bar, away from Justin and his super chic friends and his perfectly put together party.

I didn't belong there.

Even in these trendy new clothes that Laura insisted are sexy, fashionable, and worth the four hundred dollars I shelled out to purchase them, I'd felt like a lump of mashed potatoes in a room full of artisanal organic salad. Yes, mashed potatoes can offer sustenance, and are a cozy, comforting, familiar addition to any holiday meal. But compared to a fresh, crisp, perfectly proportioned salad with ginger zest and an antioxidant-packed dressing, they're just lumpy, bland, and sad.

I am lumpy. Bland. And sad.

And I really wish I had ignored Laura's assurances that after a few drinks and a little dancing I wouldn't feel the chill in the autumn air. Then I would have a jacket with me to put on to cover up my stupid boobs and failure cleavage.

Stupid Boobs and the Failure Cleavage. It's the world's worst band name and I am the world's worst at working what the good Lord gave me and I might as well convert to Catholicism, join a convent, and put myself out of my misery.

I'm about to give up on maintaining a stiff upper lip and sob openly into my wine, when a large hand touches the back of mine, and a deep voice asks, "Rough night?"

I glance over, seeing a vaguely familiar face.

The man on the stool beside me is nearly as large as Justin, with broad shoulders and thick muscles straining the fabric of his white, long-sleeved T-shirt. His short beard is neatly trimmed, but his dark blond hair is shaggy and hanging into his pale eyes. In the dim light of the bar, I can't tell if they're blue or green, but they're intelligent, focused, and…interested?

Maybe?

A little?

God, why can't I ever tell! What is broken inside of me that I'm incapable of figuring out when a man is flirting with me and when he's just being friendly?

"A little rough," I say, forcing a smile. "How about you?"

"Not the best, but things are starting to look up." He grins, showcasing slightly crooked front teeth. The minor flaw only accentuates the elegant angles of his symmetrical, dimple-blessed face. The man is very good looking. And he's talking to me, smiling at me, and making significant eye contact.

Empirically, the evidence points toward interest of a more-than-friendly variety, but I've been burned too many times to take anything for granted. This could just as easily be another opportunity for me to make a fool of myself as to practice flirting without saying the wrong thing.

When I extend my hand, I keep my tone light and friendly. "Libby."

"Tanner," the man says, his big hand enfolding mine. There is no sizzle or spark, but I'm not surprised. I can't remember the last time anyone but Roger made me tingle.

Since the morning I sprained my ankle in the slippery grass while leading my kids outside during a fire drill, and Asher Elementary's handsome, smart, sweet as homemade strawberry pie vice principal swooped me into his arms to carry me to the nurse's office, there has been no one but him. Roger is the object of my complete and utter fascination, and he has no idea I exist. At least, not in *that* way.

He doesn't know that I adore him. Or lust after him.

Like I said, he brought the tingles. Awareness was so thick in the air between us as he carried me through the school that I'd felt like the heroine at the end of *An Officer and a Gentleman*, when Richard Gere comes charging into the factory and carries Debra Winger out into the light, away from all the massive rolls of paper and frustrating boxes that need stacking. My kindergarten students are much more adorable than boxes that need stacking, and I love my job, but on that day, if Roger had kept walking past the nurse's office, out into the parking lot, and insisted on driving me back to his place in his Jeep Patriot for a steaming cup of hot tea and a steamier make-out session in his library, I wouldn't have put up a fight.

I know that movie is problematic for a lot of reasons—Laura is quick to let me know when I'm loving things that aren't the most pro-woman-power things to love—but I adore it. I love the way both characters just…know. In that moment it's so clear on their faces that they've found their forever person, the one they're going to be with for the rest of their lives.

Tanner is not going to be my forever person. But he seems nice, and he's certainly attractive. So maybe tonight doesn't have to be a total bust. Justin isn't interested in helping me—even though he's the one who's always insisting that he's there for me any time I need him—but maybe there's still a chance to learn a thing or two.

"So, why was your night off to a rocky start?" I shift toward Tanner, giving him a better view of the cleavage Laura assured me was going to draw men to me like helpless mosquitoes lured into a bug zapper, and try not to feel self-conscious.

"Work trouble." His gaze shifts to my chest and back up again so quickly I'm not sure it happened. It's even subtler than Justin's peek, but at least Tanner doesn't look horrified by the amount of skin I'm showing, so that's a plus. "A couple of the guys I work with live to give me shit."

I nod sympathetically. "I know the feeling. I'm a kindergarten teacher."

He laughs. "The kids give you a lot of shit?"

"No, not really," I say, returning his grin. "But there's always a couple troublemakers. You know, the kid who won't stop eating Play Dough or the little boy who crawls under the desks trying to look up the girl's skirts."

"Well, I can't really blame them." His eyes twinkle as he leans closer. "Play Dough smells good, and looking up a girl's skirt is just about the most fun there is."

I shake my head, nerves spiking as my heart

starts to beat faster.

This is it! That was a signal to escalate flirting, one so clear not even I could misunderstand it.

But what do I say in response? Should I keep it coy? Maybe a shy giggle before guiding the conversation back to his work? Should I go the more direct route and ask if there's a significant skirt in his life at the moment? Or should I take the flirting bull by the horns, touch his arm, and say something sexy like "now I'm regretting wearing pants?"

Or is that too completely raunchy? Would that send signals I don't really want to send, even if I try to make it obvious I'm teasing?

Holy mother of cannoli, just say something!

Speak! Move your mouth before he realizes that you're weird and goes looking for another woman to hit on!

My lips are parting and something is on the way out of my mouth—in moments like these, when my anxiety is running high, I'm never sure what I'm going to say until the words emerge and I've either pulled off communication or offered the conversational equivalent of a turd dropped in the middle of the dinner table—when a large, muscled arm wraps around my waist and the strangest thing happens.

Heat shoots through my midsection, rushing up to flush my cheeks and down to warm much more intimate places. Places I've assumed would only sizzle for Roger from now until the day I convince him we're meant to be, or my eventual death as an old cat lady—whichever comes first.

But now, there's no doubt about it. I'm sizzling. Burning. Longing for more possessive touches from a total stranger.

And then the stranger says in a familiar voice, "Tell me you're not scamming on my little sister right now, Nowicki. Please, tell me I'm seeing things," and I realize this is something much more disturbing than attraction to a man I don't know.

This is attraction to *Justin*. This is enjoying the way it feels to have *Justin's* arm wrapped around me, and the warmth of his front warming my back as he pulls me close. This is full-body tingles inspired by a man who is so firmly in the friend zone that I've never even considered what it might feel like to kiss him.

But I'm considering it now, and this night just got a hell of a lot more confusing.

CHAPTER
Four

Justin

I finally spot Libby inside the restaurant at the bar—and Nowicki next to her, drooling into her cleavage with his big dumb nose so close to hers it looks like he's about two seconds away from moving in for a kiss—and I see red. I see bright, shining no way are you sticking your tongue in my sweet Libby's mouth and giving her herpes or foot-and-mouth disease or swine flu or whatever else a knuckle-dragger like Nowicki might have floating around in that mouth-breather mouth of his, and lose it.

I bolt across the bar, wrapping my arm around Libby's waist and pulling her out of harm's way.

I draw her tight against me and bark something at Nowicki over her head. I honestly have no idea what I'm saying, just that I'm pissed and that he needs to go. Now. So I can talk to

Libby and straighten this out before she makes a serious mistake. She's way too good for Tanner. Head and shoulders out of his league, even if she is barely five three.

"Relax, man." Nowicki lifts his hands at his sides. "I had no idea she was your sister. Seriously."

"She's not my sister." I scowl at him as I hug Libby closer. Damn, she feels good. Warm and soft and curvy, she fits right beneath my chin like she was made to press against me while I yell at people over her head.

"You just said she was your sister," Nowicki says, doing that "making no sense" thing he does so well.

"I did not."

"You did." Libby's fingers curl around the arm I've got wrapped around her waist. "You said I was your little sister."

"*Like* a little sister," I amend, figuring that's probably what I said.

"No, you didn't," Libby and Tanner say at the same time. And then they have the gall to laugh together, as if they've had time to establish the kind of private jokes Libby and I have shared since we were kids.

"Well, that's what I meant." My gaze drills into Tanner's. "And that means she's off-limits, Nowicki. So take your sniffing somewhere else."

"I'm tired, anyway." He tosses a twenty on the bar and nods at Libby before adding in a softer voice, "Nice meeting you, Libby. Good luck with the Play Dough eaters. I hope your night gets better."

"Good luck to you, too," Libby says. "Sorry about this."

"Not your fault," Nowicki assures her, casting a frustrated glance in my direction before turning and walking away.

"It's nothing personal, rookie," I call after him. "Family is off-limits. Everyone knows that."

But Nowicki doesn't turn around, and a second later I realize Libby is tugging at my sleeve. I release her and she turns to me with a huff. "That was rude," she snaps, but all I can think about is how pretty she looks with her cheeks pink and her eyes glittering up at me.

Which brings me to why I was chasing her down in the first place. I need to assure her that all she needs is a little confidence and she'll be swimming in dudes. I'll get myself back in her good, *friendly* graces and put this weird night behind us.

"I'm sorry." I claim the now-empty stool beside her. "I just lost it for a second. You can do so much better than Nowicki, Libs."

Her eyes go wide even as her brow furrows. "What in the world are you talking about? Tanner is gorgeous, and as far as I could tell, very nice. Funny, too."

I scowl. "Are you sure you haven't had too much to drink?"

"No, I haven't." She lifts her wine glass. "This is my third drink, and unlike Laura, I can handle my liquor just fine. Tanner was nice, which is more than I can say for you. You practically bit the man's head off for absolutely no reason."

"No reason?" I sputter. "Did you see the way he was leering at you? He looked like the wolf about to eat Red Riding Hood's rack for dinner."

"He did not," she insists. "And even if he did, that's no reason to stomp over here and yell at the man. I'm a grown woman, not some little girl who needs you to decide who I'm allowed to talk to."

I run a clawed hand through my hair, realizing she's probably right. "Fine. I'll apologize to him at practice on Monday."

"And mean it," she says, brows lifting.

"And mean it," I agree, before adding in a more conciliatory tone, "But how about I apologize to you, first? I didn't mean to be a jerk just now, or before. You took me by surprise, that's all."

Her gaze drops to her lap, sending her thick lashes spreading across her cheeks. "It's all right. Let's just forget about it."

"I don't want to forget about it. Clearly, this is something that's bothering you. But you shouldn't be stressed, Libs. You're a beautiful, sweet, funny person who's lethal with a crochet hook. The right guy is going to see that."

"No, Jus, he isn't," she says, shaking her head.

"I am the worst at boy-girl stuff. Ask Laura. I'm completely hopeless. Half the time I'm too shy to say anything to a man I like, and the other half I say something completely insane."

"You were doing fine with Tanner." Irritation flashes through me again as I remember how close Tanner's face was to Libby's.

"No, I wasn't. I was second and third guessing myself, and probably on the verge of saying something crazy. And then Tanner would have realized that I was a weirdo and run away as fast as his big, muscly legs could carry him." She pushes on before I can remark that Nowicki is actually one of the smaller guys on the offensive line. "And I didn't even *like* him. I mean, he seemed nice, but there was no spark, you know. No sizzle. You should see how ridiculous I am when I'm actually attracted to someone. I'm a hot mess. I mean, usually, anyway…"

She shakes her head hard, sending her silky hair skimming over her shoulders, making me wonder if it's as soft as it looks. How have I been her friend for so long without finding out if her hair feels like silk? Friends should know those things about each other, right? Maybe?

"Whatever." She claims her wine from the bar and takes a big gulp, her throat working as she swallows. "Like I said, let's just forget it. I shouldn't have asked, but I trust you, and you've dated so many different kinds of women that I thought you would be able to help. Even someone like me."

"Someone like you," I repeat, the words making me sad. And a little angry. I don't like hearing people talk shit about my friends. Not even if it's them doing the shit-talking. "What's that even mean, Libs?"

"Someone who's socially awkward," she mumbles, studying her fingers as they skim up and down the stem of her glass. "I know I have a few nice things going for me, but I have no idea what I'm doing, Jus. Even if I manage to bluff my way through a first date, I have no idea how to act during the second one. And I'm even more clueless about all the other stuff." She bites her lip as she spins the glass in a slow circle. "And men my age don't want to deal with a woman whose knowledge of how to rock a guy's world plateaued her junior year of college in the back of Brett Baxter's station wagon."

I frown. "Didn't Brett end up becoming a priest?"

She nods sadly, her soft brown eyes shifting back to meet mine, sending that strange, God-Libby-is-a-beautiful-woman sensation rushing through me again. "Yes, he did. That's how good I am at the other stuff. So good that men can be with me and easily decide to give up sex forever."

My lips curve. "It was a holy calling, Libs."

"For. Ev. Ver." She hits each syllable hard enough to make me wince.

"Okay, I get it." I know I'm going to regret my

next words, but hell, this is Libby, my friend, and a good person who deserves to be happy. And if she believes a little sex ed is all she needs to get her headed down the road to happily ever after, who am I to deny her? Sure, it's going to be awkward to give her tips on how to rock a guy's world, but good friends are worth stepping out of your comfort zone for.

And at least I can be sure that this weird awareness of her will fade come tomorrow morning, once I get the alcohol and fresh-breakup-angst out of my system. I've known Libby for over a decade and never felt anything but platonic affection for her. There's no reason for that to change now, just because she decided to wear a tank top.

That's not a tank top, it's an invitation to sin, and you know it.

Ignoring the voice in my head, and the fact that my cock has been semi-hard for the past half hour for reasons I would rather not think about, I take Libby's hand and give it a gentle squeeze. "Okay. I'll do it."

She looks up, eyes wide. "Do what?"

"I'll teach you about flirting and whatever else you want to know," I say, before adding in a firm, no-nonsense tone. "But there will be rules. The first being that you never tell Laura. The second that you never tell Laura. And the third that you never—"

"Tell Laura," Libby finishes, nodding.

"Agreed. It would be too embarrassing."

"I'm not worried about being embarrassed. I'm worried about her kicking my ass when she decides I've given you bad advice that's going to get you in trouble."

Libby arches a brow. "Are you going to give me bad advice that's going to get me in trouble?"

"No, I'm going to get you laid," I say, silencing the voice in my head that insists it wouldn't mind being the one doing the laying. "On the regular, with as many men as you want to take home."

She blinks faster. "Oh no, I don't want to take home a bunch of men. Just one. His name is Roger. He's the vice principal at my school. I've been interested for a long time, but he only thinks of me as a friend."

Roger. It's a stupid name, and I decide immediately that I hate this tool who doesn't have the sense to see that Libby is adorable, sexy, girlfriend material, but I force a smile and assure her, "By the time we're finished, he's going to be begging you to be his steady date."

A cautious smile curves her lips. "Really? So you don't think I'm a hopeless case?"

"No, I don't think you're a hopeless case." The usual friendly affection I feel for Libby fills my chest as her dimples pop in response to my words, making it seem okay to add, "If you weren't like a sister to me, I would totally be trying to get into your pants."

"Right." She rolls her eyes before pinning me

with a hard look. "I have another condition, okay? No lying. I don't want you to lie or flatter me, Justin. I want the truth, even if it's hard for me to hear."

But it is the truth. For tonight, anyway.

If she were a stranger with big, brown eyes, a heart-shaped mouth, and a curvy little body rocking black leather and lace, I would be doing everything in my power to get her back to my place, into my bed, and underneath me as soon as possible. The thought of Libby—tank top off, pants unbuttoned, her breath coming faster as I let my lips play across her breasts—is enough to make that semi I've had all night become a raging, throbbing condition.

And just like that, I'm suddenly hard for Libby. Rock hard. So hard that if I give her a good-bye hug, there's no way she'll be able to miss the effect she's had on me.

So instead of hugging her good-bye, I lean in, pressing a kiss to her cheek before I assure her, "No lies. I'll swing by your place tomorrow around lunchtime. We can have our first lesson before practice." Then I bail. I bail so fast that I'm off the stool and headed back toward the party before Libby's "thank you," passes her lips.

Her sweet, full lips that I want to leave bruised and swollen because I've kissed her so hard and deep and well that there will be no doubt in her mind that she's a red-hot fucking piece of ass.

But she's not a piece of ass, she's Libby, and

I'm clearly more wasted than I realized. Time to cut the scotch, load up on carbs and water, and hope I can sober up enough to avoid being completely hungover tomorrow for Libby's first lesson.

Surely I can be back to normal by then. Especially if I can find a woman willing to come home with me and finish celebrating my birthday with a large pizza and half a dozen orgasms—for her, at least. I'm a generous man, and I'm happy to spend an hour with my face buried between a woman's legs, getting her off again and again.

Anything to keep my mind off imaginary naked Libby.

But an hour later, as the party begins to wind down, I'm still alone. None of the women rubbing up against me on the dance floor arouse more than the dimmest flickers of lust, and when I finally fall into bed around midnight, I have to fight the urge to fantasize about a certain brunette's incredible breasts as I jerk off.

The struggle is real, but I manage, and drift off to sleep hoping things will be back to normal when I wake up, though deep in my gut I know that my relationship with Libby may have changed forever.

It feels like something wild has been let out of its cage, and it's not going back in without a fight.

CHAPTER Five

From the texts of Libby and Laura Collins

Libby: Good morning, sunshine. How are you feeling?

Laura: *puking green face emoji*
vampire emoji
stabbing knife emoji

Libby: You're a puking vampire who needs to be put out of your misery?

Laura: No, I'm a puking vampire. The stabby emoji was for you.
Why are you texting me at the butt crack of dawn, you freaking sadist?

Libby: It's almost noon, Drunky Mchungoverpants, and I've got an appointment in a few minutes. I just wanted to check on you before I turn off my phone.

Laura: What kind of appointment? Are you getting a massage? If so, can I come, too? I need someone to rub the toxins out of my muscles.
God, why do I ever drink, Libs? I seriously cannot handle my liquor.

Libby: You think?

Laura: Ugh. I'm sorry. It was just a shit week, and I wanted to blow off steam like a normal twenty-seven-year-old.
Can you forgive me? I didn't embarrass you too terribly, did I?

Libby: No. You told the Lyft driver that he was sexy in an ugly way—like Mick Jagger with smaller lips—but he had a sense of humor about it, and I managed to get you into bed before you passed out.
All in all, it was a good night on the babysitting end of things.

Laura: That poor man. I hope I at least tipped him well?

Libby: You gave him a twenty and a kiss on the cheek.

Laura: Good. And I'll tip you, too, little sis.

How about team suite tickets for the game next weekend? You can drink, eat your weight in crab cakes, and watch Jus kick ass on the ice, and I'll be the babysitter who gets you home safe.

Sound good?

Libby: I think so. Let me touch base with you on Monday or Tuesday and let you know for sure I don't have other plans.

Laura: Why would you have other plans?

Oh my God, did you meet someone last night?!

Shit, you did, didn't you!? The boob shirt worked its magic and you met someone and now you're going to get lots of dick and quit obsessing about Roger!

Libby: No, I didn't meet anyone!

And I am not obsessing about Roger. I like Roger. There's a difference.

Laura: Um, no, there's not. Roger is a dink, and what you need is dick.

Wear the boob shirt again this weekend to the game and I'll make sure you're in the same suite with the guys from that cybersecurity firm that hired all the super-hot new techies. They will be helpless to resist you. You'll probably get laid in the bathroom before the game is even over.

Libby: That's what you said last night, and believe me, people had NO trouble resisting. The boob shirt and I were complete failures.

Laura: No you weren't! Last night wasn't a fair test.
You were at a party with a bunch of cocky professional athletes who think they're God's gift to pussy. You wouldn't want one of them, anyway. Trust me. They're awful. Even Jus is just barely tolerable, and that's only because I've known him since we were in seventh grade and I have photographic proof of his pimple stage to bring him back down to earth when he starts being an arrogant prick.

But the sexy nerd boys will TRULY be unable to resist. You'll have them crawling on their knees, begging you for a date in no time. I swear.

Libby: I don't want sexy nerds or professional athletes. I want Roger.

Laura: Yeah, I know, but you haven't been with anyone since college, sis.
Don't you think it's time to get back in the saddle? I mean, I know having the guy you lost your virginity to decide to become a priest totally sucked, but that's no reason to completely give up on peen. Peen can be a lot of fun, you know?

Libby: I've got to go. My appointment's about to

start.

Laura: Seriously, it doesn't have to be about true love or forever, Libs. It can just be about fun, mutual enjoyment, and proving to yourself that there is absolutely nothing wrong with you. Because there isn't, you know.

Libby: I'm not having this conversation right now, La.
Go back to sleep. I'll text you later.

Laura: I mean it, Libs. You are perfectly normal and so is your poose.
I asked the woman at the place where I made you go get waxed with me, and she swore you were all A-OK down there.

Libby: OH MY GOD, YOU DIDN'T!
TELL ME YOU DIDN'T ASK A COMPLETE STRANGER ABOUT MY VAGINA, LAURA?!

Laura: She's not a stranger! She's been waxing me for almost six years. We're practically family! And she would never tell anyone.

Libby: Oh, right! But she WILL tell my SISTER all about MY VAGINA!

Laura: Can you stop screaming that word at me, please? You know I hate it.

Especially first thing in the morning.

Libby: VAGINA! VAGINA, VAGINA, VAGINA!

Laura: Fine! Be mad and aggressive with your use of the V-word, but I was just trying to help! That's what big sisters do! We help.
And then we get drunk and make you take care of us, and then we rededicate ourselves to helping even more than we did before. So come to the game with the boob shirt. Let me help you, Libs. I love you so much, and I just want you to be happy. And I know Roger is your happy-ever-after guy, but it wouldn't hurt you to have a "just for fun" guy to help build up your confidence before you go after Roger full throttle and prove to him that you are the answer to all his romantic dreams.

Libby: Grrrr…

Laura: Don't growl at me. I'm a friend. I come in peace.
And in puke.
God, I think I'm really going to puke…
Please forgive me before I have to make a run to the bathroom.

Libby: Fine, you're forgiven.
Go puke. Text you later.

Laura: xoxox
martini glass emoji
skull emoji
toilet emoji

Libby: Indeed. xoxo

CHAPTER
Six

Libby

I can never stay mad at Laura for long. She means well. And then there's the fact that I'm a dirty, filthy liar who lies, a fact I'm reminded of every time Laura mentions helping me "get back in the saddle."

The truth is that I've never been *in* the saddle, so I can't very well hop back onto it.

Brett and I made it to third base and that's it. By the time I was ready to go all the way, Brett was ready to take a vow of celibacy.

He broke the news the day after he went down on me for the first time, an act that he clearly found so repulsive that it left me with a lingering fear that there is something *not right* about my lady parts. No matter how many times I've checked things out with my hand mirror or compared my situation to the wide variety of poose available for viewing on the internet, I still have an irrational fear that I'm like the mouth of a giant evil sandworm down there. Like something from *Beetlejuice* or *Tremors* or other 1980s movies that combine the fear of massive toothed worms and things lurking beneath the sand for horrific effect.

It's silly, but I can't seem to help it.

So I suppose I should be grateful that Laura took it upon herself to get third party reassurance that my lady bits are shipshape. But the fact that my sister has picked up on my phobia without me having mentioned a word about it is so mortifying that I want to crawl under the covers and hide for a few years—or however long it takes to convince myself that my face isn't silently telegraphing "I have concerns about the adorableness of my vagina."

But I can't hide. Justin will be here any second. He texted from the sandwich shop down the street just a few minutes ago, and I have to make sure I'm ready to hit the ground running as soon as he arrives.

Scurrying around my apartment, I get out the whiteboard and a set of multi-colored markers I use when I'm brainstorming lesson plan ideas, fetch my laptop in case Jus needs to pull up visual aids on the Internet, and track down the list of concerns and proposed areas of study I jotted down last night over a cup of Sleepy Time tea.

When the coffee table is prepped for lesson time, I glance down at my outfit—brown linen pants with ruffles at the bottom paired with a brown linen pinafore dress with a sheer, long-sleeved top underneath accessorized by chunky jewelry—and consider going to change into something sexier and less me. But in the end I decide to stay as I am. Roger and I rarely cross paths outside of work hours and these are the kind of clothes I wear to teach—professional and cute, but loose-fitting enough to facilitate sitting on the floor with a roomful of kindergarteners, helping clean up blocks and toys, and scooping Simone up under one arm and running her to the girls' room down the hall when she inevitably waits too long to get in line for our classroom bathroom and is on the verge of an accident.

The poor kid. It's hard being the youngest student in class. I was homeschooled until the ninth grade, but I vividly remember how mortified I was to learn that I was the only thirteen-year-old at Capital High. But at least I'd had Justin and Laura there to show me the ropes.

And now Jus is going to show you the ropes all over again. Except this time, he's going to instruct you on the finer points of how to suck a man's cock.

My cheeks flame at the thought. The only thing that keeps them from catching fire is the knowledge that we surely won't get that far along in the lesson plan today. Like I tell my students, it's best to put first things first, and there's a lot of ground to cover before Jus and I get to anything below the belt. The valley of my ignorance is deep and wide, with acres of undiscovered country standing between me and anything that wild and uninhibited.

"And Roger might not even want to do things like that," I murmur to myself as I put the kettle on and pluck another gardenia-peach tea bag from the box. I mean, surely not every guy foams at the mouth at the thought of a woman kissing him where he pees. That's at least partly urban legend, right?

I'm about to trot into the living room to add that question to my list when the doorbell rings, setting my pulse to racing.

It's time. He's here.

I hurry to the door, anticipation and nerves mixing in my bloodstream. I try to tell myself it's not a big deal, it's just Justin, but then I open the door and he says, "Hey," in this oddly husky voice and my pulse stutters before rushing even faster.

"H-hey," I stammer, voice breathy.

I don't know what's wrong with me. I've looked into those dreamy hazel eyes a thousand times before and never felt anything more than affection for an old friend. But now I'm newly aware of the handsome planes of his face, the silkiness of his nearly-black brown hair, and the way his shoulders seem to take up the entire doorframe. I can't keep from staring at his big hand gripping that brown sandwich bag, and thinking about what it felt like to have that hand pressed flat against my fluttering stomach last night.

I had assumed the tingle attack at the bar was an anomaly brought on by a mixture of dating-related despair and too much alcohol, but maybe I was wrong.

And maybe these lessons are going to be even more awkward than I expected.

CHAPTER
Seven

Libby

"Should I come in?" Jus nods meaningfully toward me, making it clear I've been standing here staring at him for too long.

"Yes, of course. Sorry." I move out of the way with a nervous laugh, flapping my hand toward the kitchen on the other side of my microscopic entryway. "Can I get you something to drink? Tea or water or juice?"

"Still anti-soda?" He shrugs off his coat as he moves inside, sending a whiff of his Justin scent drifting my way. He smells even better than he did last night—a combo of soap, fresh air, sea salt, and a hint of toasted bread from the sandwich shop that sort of makes me want to bite him. It's a completely foreign urge, one that is shocking enough to make me stumble over the welcome mat as I close the door.

"You okay?" Jus asks, arching a brow.

"Fine. Two left feet, as usual." I ignore the mouthwatering smell of him and head to the fridge. "And yes, I'm still anti-soda, but I've got sparkling fruit-flavored things. Orange or cranberry; choose your poison."

"That's all right. I'll stick with tea," he says, holding out his paper bag. "I brought you half of my second sandwich. You still love the Vietnamese veggie, right?"

"Yes, thank you." I accept the bag and tuck my future dinner onto the top shelf before shutting the fridge and turning back to him, feeling off-center in a way I've never felt around Jus. "That was thoughtful."

"No problem." He nods a little too long, his gaze fixed on the tile, before he sucks in a deep breath and lets it out with a sigh. "So, I've been thinking about this, Libs…"

"Yes?" My throat tightens. "Please don't tell me that you've changed your mind."

"I mean, of course I want to help you, but I have no idea where to start, and—"

"That's okay!" I say with forced brightness. "I made a list last night and I've got study materials all ready in the living room. That should get us started, and then we can just let the lesson plan flow from there. I'm good at lesson plans, and you're good at getting people to date you, so this should really be a no-brainer."

"Right. Okay." But he still refuses to lift his

gaze from whatever fascinating thing is happening next to my feet, and when he speaks again he sounds as uncomfortable as I feel. "So what's the first thing on the list?"

"I can't remember. I'll have to look at my notes. You want to wait in the living room and I'll get the tea ready? You're still Earl Grey with extra sugar, right?"

"Yeah, thanks." He casts a longing glance toward the door before reluctantly moving toward the living room.

As soon as he's out of sight, I squeeze my eyes shut and give myself a silent pep talk—

Stop being crazy! Stop it! Right now! This is Justin.

So you're feeling weird fizzy things around him. So what? It doesn't matter.

He's a drop-dead gorgeous professional hockey player who lives up to his bad-boy, womanizing reputation, and you're the world's oldest virgin elementary school teacher. He's a shark who roams the open sea banging all the sexiest, most beautiful and successful female sharks, and you're a goldfish who's never been out of your bowl.

He's so far out of your league he might as well be another species, Libby, and even if he weren't, he would still be completely off-limits. He's practically family and has already mentioned several times that he thinks of you as a little sister.

Besides, Roger is the one you want. This is just physical weirdness, nothing that can't be overcome.

So get in there, push through the awkward part, and get the information you need. New things are never easy, but you can't afford to screw up what might be your only chance to turn your non-existent love life around.

Bolstered by the wisdom of the inner voice, I arrange the tea things on a tray and carry them into the living room to find Justin standing by my craft nook in the corner, flipping through a pattern book.

He turns, glaring at me over his shoulder as he holds up *May the Force Be Knit You.* "How was this not my birthday present, Collins? Star Wars crochet and knitting patterns? My inner yarn nerd is freaking the hell out right now."

"Take it, it's yours." I laugh at the pure delight that flashes across his face. "I've got so many projects lined up I won't get around to anything new until next Christmas, anyway." I set the tray down on the coffee table. "And I'm sure your followers will go wild over a shot of you wearing nothing but Yoda ears."

"Or Wookie gloves." He flips through the pages as he flops down onto the couch beside me. "Or Jabba the Hutt fat folds! Jesus Christ, Libs, did you know you could crochet your own ring of neck fat folds? I need to get online and order some of this nasty red-orange yarn right now."

I giggle, grateful for the reminder that Justin is as much of a complete dork as I am. He may be a shark on the outside, but on the inside he's got a little goldfish in him. It's why we're every bit as close as he and Laura are, and why this is going to be completely fine. I just need to remember his goofiness and forget I ever noticed that he is just as hot as the ice bunnies who hang around the arena after the games say he is.

"I'll order it for you myself, my treat." I grab my spiral notebook and tuck my socked feet beneath me. "As soon as we're done with lesson one."

"All right, let's do this." He tosses the pattern book onto the coffee table, clearly eager to get down to business now that there's a reward involved. He lifts his hands, curling his fingers in a come-and-get-me way. "Hit me."

"Okay." I glance down, clicking my pen. "Number one. What to talk about on a first date."

Jus chews the inside of this cheek the way he does when he's figuring out a particularly difficult line of a crochet pattern, proving he intends to bring some real thought to this. "I think a better question is what *not* to talk about on a first date. Most guys are forgiving when it comes to the small talk being a little forced at first. But hit them with something freaky fresh out of the gate and you're going to have a hell of a time getting the dude to return a text, let alone sign on for date two."

"Right." I flip to a clean sheet of paper and poise my pen over the page. "So what *don't* I talk about? No big feelings, right?"

"Absolutely. No big feelings. I mean, if you're

passionate about a hobby or something that's fine, but nothing that might signal that you're high maintenance. Save feelings for the third or fourth date, and keep those light. Before that, absolutely keep your emotional state to yourself."

I nod as I quickly jot down a few notes. "Okay. But I think my emotional state is actually pretty solid. I mean, I get nervous with new people and in unfamiliar situations, but once I'm comfortable, I'm pretty low maintenance."

"True," Jus agrees. "But your new guy won't know that. And if you've been mooning over him for a long time, he'll probably be skittish. Especially at first."

I prickle. "I haven't been mooning over him. Roger has no idea I like him. I've been very subtle."

Justin snorts. "Yeah, because you're *soooo* subtle, Libs."

"I can be!"

"Um, sorry. No," he says, a smug grin curving his lips. "Everything you feel shows on your face, babes. If you're thinking it, the entire world knows about it."

My cheeks flush so hot I know my face must be turning bright red. "That's not true," I protest, though I'm silently dying inside, the fear that everyone knows that I have zero confidence in my dating abilities, and nearly as little in the normalcy of my vagina, returns with a vengeance.

"It is," Jus insists, leaning closer. "Right now,

for example, you're worried everyone knows that you're anxious about dating."

"I am not!" I cross my arms at my chest with a huff and glare up at his stupid face. "I was wishing I'd made coffee, instead of tea, and thinking about how weird it is that you get your eyebrows waxed."

He laughs. "Liar. And I don't get my eyebrows waxed. I get them threaded at this little Indian salon around the corner from the arena. They do great work, only make me cry a little bit. Tiny little man tears."

I press my lips tight together. "I'm not going to laugh at you. This isn't funny. All you've done so far is make me even more self-conscious. Let's assume you're right, and everything I think does show on my face. What am I supposed to do about it? Wear a bag over my head for the rest of my life?"

"No, of course not," Jus says, his grin fading. "You don't have to do anything about it, Libs. You're an open, honest person, and that's great. You just need to up your confidence level and you'll be fine. And that's what we're doing, right? So you're already on the road to success."

"We'll see," I grumble, clicking my pen twice in rapid succession. "What else shouldn't I talk about?"

Justin quickly ticks off warnings about politics, religion, money, and a few other no-brainers before going more in depth. "Don't talk about if you want kids or how many. Don't talk about ex-boyfriends or dark secrets or your crazy family or your favorite sexual positions."

My eyebrows shoot up. "People really talk about that? On the first date?"

"Oh hell, yes, they do. I once had a girl tell me over the appetizer course that she could only come if she got it hard from behind, doggie style, and then only with a guy who was packing at least eight or nine solid inches." He shrugs. "I guess she wanted me to know what she was looking for before she wasted time with small talk."

"Wow." I blink, unable to imagine having a conversation like that with anyone. Ever. Let alone while I was trying to eat. "That's, um… So what did you do?"

"What did I do?" he echoes.

"Yeah. You said sexual positions aren't something I should talk about on a first date. So what did you do after this girl broke the code?"

"Oh, well…" He rolls his shoulder uncomfortably. "That doesn't really matter. Just know that it isn't a solid choice for a beginner."

Now it's my turn to smirk. "You took her home, didn't you?"

He clears his throat. "Maybe."

"Yes, you did. You took her home. And then you dated her, didn't you?" I ask with a laugh, something prickling at the back of my mind. "Oh my God, it was Cindy, wasn't it? Cindy, the girl who had the donkey laugh, but who was really nice, with the pretty red hair!"

"Fine. Yes, it was Cindy." He rolls his eyes. "And yes, she was nice and I liked her. But being told on the first date how she preferred to get fucked wasn't what made it work for as long as it did."

"Why did you guys break up?'"

"I'd rather not say," he says, running a hand through his hair.

"Please tell me?" I beg, sensing there is something to be learned from that part of the story, too. "I promise I won't tell anyone or tease you about it."

His sighs. "She cheated on me. She found a guy with a ten-inch dick that she preferred to mine and moved on."

"I'm sorry," I say, even as my brain begins to unpack his words and do the associated math.

"Don't." He points a warning finger at my face. "I see what you're doing there, Collins."

I shake my head, fighting a smile. "I'm not doing anything."

"Yes, you are. You're making guesses about how many inches I've got, and that is none of your business. All you need to know is that it's more than enough to keep a woman happy. In case any of your cute single friends decide they're in need of a highly satisfying and pleasurable one-night stand while I'm on the rebound. Message received?"

"Received." I nod in surrender, wondering

how many times I'm going to blush rutabaga red before we're finished with lesson one. At this rate, I'll have to invest in ice compresses before we start lesson two. "Moving on, then?"

"Moving on," he agrees, still scowling, but in a way that makes it obvious he's not seriously upset. Clearly he's over Cindy and still quite confident in his abilities in the bedroom, which is exactly why he's the perfect person for this job.

He really is perfect and a very good friend. "I'll crochet the fat folds for you myself if you want. I really am so grateful."

Jus grins. "Nah, I'll do it myself. Getting there is half the fun, right?"

"Right," I agree, beginning to think this might be fun, too. Or at least not as painful as I'd assumed. But then, I've always had fun with Justin. He's good at fun and I'm much better at it when I'm with him.

CHAPTER *Eight*

Justin

L ibby puts a big check mark beside the first item on her list, apparently feeling confidant in her ability to make conversation that doesn't tread into dangerous-for-a-first-date territory. She's very cute with her lists and her questions, though I'm still having a hard time taking this completely seriously. Yes, I get that she hasn't dated much since college, but Libby is a perfectly normal person. All she needs to do is be herself, and good things—and good dating relationships—should follow.

But if talking through this stuff with me is making her feel better, I can kill a few hours sipping tea and talking shop. There are worse ways to spend an afternoon than catching up with an old friend, who is also going to set you up with the sweetest pattern book ever.

I'm just glad the weirdness from last night is gone.

Today, Libby is once again dressed like Libby, in a combination of loose linen clothing that makes her resemble an oversize Raggedy Ann doll, and the vibe between us is back to being purely friendly.

Sure, maybe I noticed that the shirt she's wearing beneath her dress is see through, and grants the focused man a tiny peek of cleavage when she bends over. And maybe I noticed how cute her feet are in the lacy socks she's wearing, and the way her eyes flashed when she was guessing how many inches I'm packing, but overall things are back to normal and I seem to be helping.

I'm feeling pretty good about myself when she says, "Number two: Transitions," and I frown, wondering if there's something I've overlooked in my ten-plus years of dating.

"What kind of transitions?" I claim my mug from the tray.

"You know, like from the first date to the second date." She glances down at her notepad as she adds, "Or from kissing to something more than kissing. That's the part I'm most concerned about, honestly. It can be hard to move smoothly from the first part to…the other parts. You know? Sometimes?"

"Oh. Okay." I nod, taking a drink of tea to stall for time.

Hard to get from the first part to the other parts? What is she even talking about? It's like she's asked me what to do after she exhales. You inhale. And then you exhale. And then you inhale again.

Seriously. It's as natural as breathing, isn't it?

"I mean, I know it doesn't have to be awkward," she says, clearly sensing my confusion. "With Brett things were fine, but I'd known him since ninth grade. We were friends for a long time before we were anything more and it just…" She shrugs as she wags her pen nervously back and forth. "It flowed, you know? But since then, every time I'm with someone and things start to get more intense it starts feeling forced and awkward and I end up making an excuse to leave."

I shake my head, still mystified. "Maybe it's the guys you're going out with? Maybe they're not the—"

"No, it's me," she breaks in, dropping her notepad and pen onto the coffee table before lifting her hands into the air. "Like, with my hands. I never know what to do with my hands. And then I get stressed out and I can't figure out what to do with my arms, either. And before I know it, I'm tense and in my head and either lying there like a chunk of petrified wood while my date does his best to move things along without me, or jumping up and running for the door like a spazz."

I nod again, a sick feeling spreading through my stomach.

Jesus. Poor Libby. I'm beginning to think maybe she does need sex education classes after all, and to suspect that my sweet friend is probably really, *really* bad in bed.

"Oh God." Her forehead wrinkles. "You think I'm a freak, too."

"No, I don't. I'm just thinking."

"Thinking that I'm a freak who is less fun in bed than a blow-up doll," she says, her big brown eyes beginning to shine. "I mean, at least a blow-up doll doesn't accidentally hit you in the face while she's trying to take her shirt off and give you a nosebleed and a black eye. And yes, that really happened. In my defense, it was a really tight turtleneck and my palms were sweaty, but still. I'm a freak."

I fight a smile. "You're not a freak. You're just overthinking things. You let a couple bad experiences throw you, and now you're sabotaging yourself before you even get started. It's like a couple years ago, when I missed a shot into a wide open net at the season opener. The goalie offered it to me on a silver platter and I fucked it up. And for the next two weeks, I couldn't score a goal to save my life. Every time I went to shoot, for a split second I'd think about the shot I missed, and that was all it took to throw my game."

"But you eventually got over it," she says

softly. "How?"

"Meditation," I confess, though I've never told anyone but Brendan how hard I had to work to get my stupid brain back in line. But Libs isn't judgmental and she understands what it's like to royally psych herself out. "I took private lessons. Even got up at five a.m. a couple of times so I could get a class in before practice. After about a week, I was shooting straight again. Now I meditate before every game, between every period, and any other time I need to get sharp."

"So you think I should meditate before second base?" she asks, arching a brow.

"No." I laugh as I set down my mug. "I think you should meditate before you get ready to go out. Just close your eyes, concentrate on your breath, and visualize the date going the way you want it to go."

Libby's nose wrinkles. "You think that will work?"

I nod. "Hockey and sex actually have a lot in common."

"They do?" She eyes me skeptically as I take her gently by the shoulders and urge her to lean back against the couch cushions.

"They do. They're both very reactive sports."

"Sports?" She snorts. "That says a lot about you, Jus."

"Pastimes, then," I amend. "They can both be fast-paced and unpredictable." I shift to sit on the edge of the coffee table, facing Libby. "That's why it's important to stay in the moment. To breathe and relax and be ready to respond at a second's notice."

Her lips press together as she nods slowly. "Okay. How do I do it?"

"Close your eyes," I say softly, nodding when she hesitates. "Go ahead. Close 'em." She obeys with a wrinkle of her nose. "Good. Now roll your shoulders back, relax your jaw, and let go as you concentrate on your breath. As you inhale, visualize calm flowing into your body like a white cloud. And as you exhale imagine tension streaming out in a yellow puff of smoke."

"Can it be a gray puff? When I think smoke, I think gray."

"Sure, gray smoke is fine," I say, lips curving as Libby wiggles deeper into the cushions. "In with the white, out with the gray. In with white, out with gray, gently bringing your thoughts back to the breath when they try to break off and go somewhere else."

She nods and her shoulders relax a little farther away from her ears.

"If other thoughts or fears or worries arise," I continue in a soft, even voice, "notice them, acknowledge them—yes, thoughts about what I need to pick up at the store, or how dumb it is to sit here doing nothing but breathe, I see you, there you are—and then go back to your breath without judgment. Don't let your mind get attached to anything but the breath. The breath is the only sticky thing, everything else floats in and floats out."

Libby sighs and shifts again, but after a few moments, her breath is coming in longer and smoother waves and the tension has melted from her features, making me think she's found her ground zero. I think of that quiet, focused place as my launch pad, the spot where I go to shut out the world before I get down to the work that happens between the ears.

"Once you feel like the slate is clean, go ahead and imagine you're getting ready to go out with old Roger."

"He's not old," she says in a calm, Zenned-out voice. "He's only thirty-two."

"So you're getting ready for a date with not-old Roger," I amend, silently disagreeing with Libby. Eight years makes more of a difference than most people think, and what's wrong with Roger that he's still single at thirty-two? Don't most schoolteacher types get married a lot younger than that?

"Okay, I'm getting ready," Libby says, breaking into my admittedly judgmental thoughts. She still sounds chill, which is good. It took me a few sessions before I could stay in my happy place while visualizing or responding to questions.

"What are you doing?" I ask.

"I'm taking a shower, washing my hair."

"Good, concentrate on the slippery feel of the

shampoo, and the way your hair glides through your fingers when it's wet." I'm winging it a little bit—my meditation exercises are all focused on staying in my body while I'm on the ice—but I figure encouraging her to pay attention to sensual, tactile details will get her in a better frame of mind for imagining a smooth transition from making out to something more. "Can you feel it?"

"I can." She lifts her chin. "I can feel the water hot on my chest. The air is warm and humid, but in a good way."

"Good." A mental picture of Libby, naked, with water streaming over her flushed skin, flashes through my head, stirring things in places where they shouldn't be stirring.

Time to get imaginary Libby out of the fucking shower.

I swallow hard. "So now you're clean and relaxed. What do you do next?"

"I get dressed, letting my hair dry by the fireplace while I put my makeup on. I put on my happy, sunny day playlist and have a glass of wine."

"And you feel good, confidant," I prod. "You look beautiful, and you're going to blow Roger's socks off."

Her lips curve. "I do feel pretty."

"Beautiful," I insist, because she is. Given the chance to sit here and study her full pink lips, gently sloped nose, and thick lashes spread out across her cheeks, there's no arguing the point.

Libby is beautiful, so stunning that some man should have fucking noticed by now. They should have been able to see past the baggy clothes and Lib's natural shyness to the stunning woman waiting for someone to show her that she's as sexy as she wants to be.

"All right," she whispers. "I'm beautiful. And when I meet Roger at the restaurant he looks at me the way I've always wanted him to look at me."

"Of course he does," I agree, ignoring the irrational voice that is annoyed by the fact that the starring role in her fantasy is played by an idiot. He has to be an idiot. If he weren't, he would have given Libs a chance by now. "And dinner goes well. You talk, you laugh, and he realizes how amazing you are."

"We talk about work and school," she says dreamily. "Then we talk about our families, and skiing, and how much we love to get on a lift at night, when the snow is all blue in the moonlight and it feels like you're flying over the treetops."

"The best time to ski in the world."

"Like magic." She smiles. "I can't wait for the first snow."

"Me, either," I say, hoping I get the chance to ski with Libs this season. Last year I was so busy with work and entertaining my woman of the moment—Bethany, the girl between Sylvia and Cindy, who had a fit every time I neglected to call her while I was at an away game—that I didn't make it up to the mountains a single time. But instead of telling Libby that I need her to drag me up to Mt. Hood before December, I reluctantly return to the task at hand. "Now, dinner is over and everything is going well. What happens next?"

"We go for a walk through the city," she says. "He offers me his coat and it smells like him."

"What does he smell like?"

She cocks her head. "A little like the cafeteria, because school cafeteria smell never completely comes out of wool, but mostly like cologne and grass and the air right before it snows."

"Nice." Ugh. Not nice. Repulsive is more like it. My irrational loathing for Roger grows with every word out of her pretty mouth, but still I ask, "And how do you feel while you're walking?"

"Good. Relaxed, but excited, too. He holds my hand and I know that we're going to kiss soon, but I'm not afraid."

"Keep going," I encourage, forcing myself to keep my tone soft and supportive, even as I realize I really don't want to hear about how fucking amazing it is to make out with Roger. I don't want to hear Libby talk about kissing anyone, honestly.

But you would like to know what she tastes like, what it feels like when her lips part and she lets you into her mouth.

I clear my throat, fighting another rogue wave of awareness as Libby starts to speak in this husky

73

voice that does nothing to stem the tide.

"We stop on a deserted street corner near the park. Everything is quiet. It's late on a weeknight and we're alone. I look up at him and tell him that I want to be more than friends." Her eyelids flutter like they do in REM sleep, but remain closed, making me think her visualization is getting pretty intense. "He says he feels the same way and then he kisses me."

"What's it like?" I ask, my body responding to the sexy way she drags her teeth over her bottom lip in response.

"His lips are warm and his arms are tight around me, but not too tight." Her breath starts to come faster as she adds, "And now I'm putting my arms around his neck and he keeps kissing me and then…"

"And then?" This is turning into an exercise in torture, but I can't help myself. I want to hear what happens next. I want to know what it feels like when she lets a kiss become something more.

"And then, I…" Her tongue slips out, wetting her lips. "And then I start to get stiff, tighten up."

"No, you don't, Libby."

"Yes, I do." Her brow furrows. "I remember that we're on a sidewalk in the middle of the city. We're not really alone. Someone might see us. I try to tell Roger, but—"

"No one's going to see. This is your world. You're calling the shots."

"No, I'm not." She shakes her head. "And

now I just bit Roger's tongue! Oh my God, now he's bleeding and looking at me like I'm crazy. Like I did it on purpose!"

"No, no, no. Hit rewind, Libs." I scoot closer, until our knees almost touch. "Hit stop and rewind. Everything was going fine, you just need to relax."

"I can't," she says, her breath rushing out. "I'm the worst kisser ever, and Roger is going to file assault charges. I'm going to end up in jail, and it's your fault for building up my confidence and making me a menace to society."

I fight a laugh. "Don't be ridiculous, Libs."

"Don't laugh at me!"

"I'm not, I'm not. Just focus on your breath again," I say, doing my best to get her back on the rails. "Concentrate on long, slow inhalations and—"

"I can't." Her voice breaks, and her next words emerge in a sob. "It's over. I screwed it up. God, I can't even *imagine* it right. What's wrong with me?"

And in that moment, I realize that if I'm going to convince Libby to trust her instincts, then I have to trust mine. And every one of mine is screaming to fuck the meditation session and go for a more…hands-on approach.

CHAPTER
Nine

Justin

Before my brain has the chance to second-guess my gut, I lean in, cutting off Libby's next words with a kiss.

She sucks in a surprised breath. I take advantage of the moment, sweeping my tongue across her bottom lip, getting my first taste of her. And from that first explosion of honey, flowers, tea, and woman spreading across my tongue, I know Libby Collins is one of the sweetest things I'll ever taste.

"Justin…" My name is a soft warning, but her fingers thread into my hair, her nails dragging lightly across the skin at the back of my neck, leaving no doubt that Libby has excellent instincts.

All she needs is a little practice.

"Kiss me, Libby," I say, my hand sliding over

the curve of her hip.

"But—"

This time, I stroke deep between her lips, moaning in approval as her tongue begins to dance with mine. At first, she's shy—teasing, testing—but by the time I join her on the couch, she's giving as good as she gets, and there is absolutely nothing wrong with her technique. Her lips are firm and hot and the sound she makes when my hand skims up her ribs to hover below her breast is sexy enough to make me instantly, painfully hard.

"What are you doing?" Her nails dig deeper into my skin.

"What does it feel like I'm doing?" I nip her bottom lip as I brush my thumb back and forth, caressing the soft curve of her breast.

Her chest rises and falls faster, making my cock throb. Getting a woman turned on is always an aphrodisiac like no other, but getting Libby turned on is hot as fucking hell. I want to drive her crazy, to see what happens when she lets go and lets herself feel without anxiety throwing on the brakes.

"We can't," she whispers, but when I brush my thumb over her nipple through her clothes, she doesn't pull away.

She gasps, a sexy cry that I swallow as I kiss her again.

I kiss her harder, deeper, until her breath is coming fast and she's arching into the hand I've kept lingering below her breast. I wait until she moans, a hungry, needy sound that's meaning is perfectly fucking clear, before I wrap my arms around her, pulling her on top of me as I lie back on the couch.

"Spread your legs," I murmur against her lips, cursing beneath my breath as she obeys, bringing her center into intimate contact with where I'm insanely hard for her. "Do you feel that, Libs?"

"Yes." She rocks experimentally against me in a way that makes my vision blur, and it's almost impossible to keep from fusing my mouth to hers again immediately.

But I force myself to wait, needing her to understand what she does to me, to own the power she has in this moment.

"That's because I want you. So fucking much." I grip her ass firmly in my right hand, encouraging her to keep moving, to keep riding me through our clothes while I tell her how hot she is. "Because you're sexy as hell, and all I want to do is get you out of these clothes and get inside you. And all you've done is kiss me, Libby. That's it. That's all it took to get me wild for you."

Her forehead presses against mine as she grinds her hips in these little circles that quickly drive me out of my mind. "We shouldn't be doing this."

"Doing what?" I bring my hand back to her breast, capturing her nipple through the thin linen and squeezing the puckered flesh between my fingers. "Dry humping on your couch?"

"Gross. That makes it sound disgusting, Justin." She drags her teeth over my bottom lip in what I gather is supposed to be a punishment, but only makes me hotter.

"And see there? You bit me and no one's bleeding." I guide the strap of her dress down her shoulder. "In fact, I'd like it if you bit me some more. Would you like a list of all the places I'd like for you to bite me?"

"No," she says, breath coming faster.

"Fine, then I'll tell you all the places *I* want to bite *you*."

"No, we—" Her words end in a sharp inhalation as I slip my hand under her shirt and up her bra, finding her bare nipple. And fuck, her skin is soft and hot and that sweet little tip is so hard all I want to do is to get it in my mouth.

"Right here." I dig my fingers into her ass as I tease her tip with whisper soft brushes of my thumb. "First I'll lick your nipple, suck you in my mouth until you're begging me for more, and then I'll bite you. Right here." I pinch her tight, and she responds by rocking against my cock hard enough to make my head explode.

"Fuck, Libby, you make me so hot." I haul her mouth back to mine, kissing her so hard our teeth grind against each other through our lips, while she writhes on top of me, growing wilder with every kiss, every touch, every roll of her nipple between my fingers.

It isn't long before my cock is desperate for relief, weeping sad, lonely tears of pre-come and insisting he's going to suffocate if I don't get out of these fucking jeans. But this isn't about me, or him; it's about showing Libby she's not the slightest bit weird or broken.

Somewhere in my lust-fogged head, I know she's right. We shouldn't be doing this. This is not good or wise, but who cares about good or wise when a beautiful woman is about to come? It doesn't matter that we're both still fully clothed and that I know I won't be joining her. I still want Libby's orgasm. I still crave the sound of her crying out because I got her off, because I gave her bliss and release and took control and made her sweet body do my bidding.

"Come for me, Libs," I murmur into the shell of her ear as I gather her hair in my free hand, wanting to see her face when she goes. "Ride me until you fucking explode, babes."

She shakes her head, but her cheeks are pink and her lips are already forming that "Oh, God" O-shape I know so well. I've seen it on the faces of more than my share of women, but I can't remember the last time the sight of a woman on the brink made me this crazy, this desperate.

I need her orgasm, need it more than my next fucking breath.

I fist my fingers in her thick, silky hair, holding her still as I move my other hand to her ass, gripping the firm flesh of her bottom as I draw her pussy tighter to my cock. "That wasn't a question, Libby." I rock against her with smooth, controlled rolls of my hips, making sure the ridge of my erection is giving her clit everything I've got. "You're going to come for me. You're going to come so hard you're going to have to change your panties when we're done they're going to be so fucking wet."

"I can't," she gasps, hands pressed tight to my chest. "Oh God, Justin, I can't. I can't do this."

Before I can insist that she can and she will—I won't settle for anything less than her complete and profound release—she slips out of my arms. A moment later, she's on her feet, running out of the living room.

"Libby, wait!"

I'm answered by a slamming door and a muffled plea. "Go away!"

I jump to my feet, wincing as I pause to adjust myself in my suddenly way-too-tight jeans, and hurry to her bedroom. I knock lightly on the closed door. "Come on, Libby, let me in. Let's talk."

But there is no response. I call her name again and again. I do a shitty job of apologizing, and then apologize again for being shitty at saying "I'm sorry" for almost making her come, but she doesn't say a word.

I'm about to pop the lock on the door with an Allen wrench I found in her junk drawer—just to make sure she's okay in there—when my phone buzzes in my back pocket.

It's a text from Libby telling me that she's gone and that by the time she comes back I should be, too, giving me proof positive that I've royally fucked up.

CHAPTER Ten

Justin

At practice I suck harder than I've sucked since my rookie season, when for a little while I wasn't sure I had what it took to skate with the big boys.

I miss half the pucks during passing drills, give up a shorthanded goal while quarterbacking a power play, and fall on my fucking face after botching a slap shot during the final scrimmage. By the time coach calls practice at a quarter 'til eight my body is nearly as bruised as my pride, and I head for the tunnel with a dark cloud hanging over my head. In the locker room, a pair of smartass blueliners ask if I missed my nap today, and Schwartz shouts that he hasn't seen stick work like mine since he left the minors.

I'm about to tell him to take his stick and shove it up his ass when Nowicki has the nerve to defend me, telling Schwartz, "Shut the fuck up. Everyone has a bad day every once in a while."

"I don't need your pity, rookie," I snap, shoving my shoulder pads into my locker with more force than necessary. "Keep your Boy Scout shit to yourself."

"Fine. Fuck you, too." Nowicki shrugs out of his jersey, muttering something foul beneath his breath, and out of nowhere I hear Libby's voice in my head, telling me not to be an asshole.

It isn't Nowicki's fault that my focus was for shit today, and I did promise Libs that I would apologize to Tanner for being a dick at my party. Besides, as my shit show of a practice so helpfully reminded me, it isn't easy being a rookie. Nowicki might have a touch of ADHD, but he works hard and he's having a solid first season. He's going to be an asset to the Badgers long term, and could probably use a little encouragement as much as the next newbie.

"Hey, Nowicki…" I take a deep breath. "I'm sorry. And sorry I chewed your ass last night. Libby's been my friend since we were kids. I saw you two talking close and I overreacted."

Nowicki frowns, studying me out of the corner of his eye like he's waiting for the punch line of a bad joke.

"I'm serious," I continue. "You did good work out there tonight. And at the last game. Keep it up and you're going to see more ice time. No doubt."

"Thanks," he says, cautiously. "And I wasn't trying anything with your friend. We were just talking."

"You were drooling on her chest, man. Don't push it."

His lips quirk. "Well, you can't blame a man for looking."

"Oh, yes, I can," I say, temper flaring. Nowicki wasn't just looking, he was thinking about touching, and after this afternoon, the thought of anyone else's hands on Libby makes me want to put a fist through a wall. Or maybe Nowicki's fucking baby face. "You don't look at her again, asshole. I'm serious."

"Hey, she could do worse." Tanner backs toward the showers with his hands lifted in surrender. "I'm a nice guy, Cruise. And you know what they say about nice guys."

"They finish last?" I snap as I wrap my towel tight around my hips.

"They get the good stuff in the end. There are rewards for being there to pick up the pieces after a girl's been screwed over by the dicks of the world," he says, a smug grin curving his lips. "A grateful pussy is a beautiful thing."

"Go. Shower. Right now. Before I remember how much I really don't like you."

Nowicki laughs and ambles toward the steam rising from the other side of the room. I'm still debating whether or not to stick my sweaty jockstrap in his helmet as punishment for talking about Libby's pussy, even in a sneaky roundabout way, when Brendan appears beside me, already showered and in street clothes.

"You need to talk?" he asks, his forehead furrowed and his blue eyes looking genuinely concerned.

"No." I slam my locker closed. "Just having an off day."

"You sure? Seemed like something was under your skin. Or in your head. You still seeing that shrink?"

"She's a meditation expert, not a shrink," I grumble. "And no, I haven't been in a while. But that's not what's wrong. I just…" I stretch my head to one side, fighting the knot forming in my neck. "Just had a weird afternoon. Some crazy shit went down with a friend, and I didn't have a chance to talk things through and figure out what happens next, you know? She just bailed and told me to get lost and now…" I sigh. "Fuck, I don't know."

Brendan nods slowly. "So you and Laura finally slept together?"

"What?" I frown so hard it sends a flash of pain through my skull. "Hell, no. Jesus! Why would you even say something like that?"

He shrugs. "There's a lot of sexual tension between you two."

"Ew. Gross. No, there isn't. There is no sexual tension between Laura and me. Just thinking about it is enough to keep my dick soft until

Christmas." I shudder, genuinely repulsed. After this afternoon, there is only one Collins sister on my radar, and that's one too many. Kissing Libs, touching her, talking dirty to her while she rocked on my cock was a mistake.

One I have no idea how to bounce back from. I'm pretty sure showing up on her doorstep wearing nothing but one of the socks she knitted me in high school on my dick and a sign around my neck that says "my cock is in time out until he remembers how to act with friends," probably isn't a good idea. In fact, showing up wearing nothing but a sock sends the opposite fucking message, proving no part of me is thinking straight right now.

"Whatever you say," Brendan says, clearly not convinced. "But if you want to talk, I'm around. Sometimes getting whatever's messing with your head out into the open is enough to keep it off the ice, you know?"

"I know. Shit." I squeeze my eyes shut, cursing softly again before I confess, "It's Libby. I went over to her place to give her some advice today and things got way out of hand."

I give Brendan a brief rundown of the situation, knowing he's a vault and would never tell anyone that Libby asked me to give her a crash course on sex and dating, or share that I proved to be the kind of perverted professor who can't keep his hands off of his student.

"No clothes came off," I add in a hushed

voice, not wanting anyone else to overhear. "But we were headed there fast when all of sudden she bailed. She bolted for her bedroom and a few minutes later I got a text saying she'd crawled out the fire escape because she needed to be alone and that she would prefer not to see me or talk to me for at least a year. Maybe more."

Brendan scratches beneath his jaw as he lets out a long, slow breath. "Wow. That's…not good."

"No, it's not. And she won't respond to any of my texts or answer my calls and I feel like shit. I was supposed to help her, and all I did was make her more upset." I lean back against my locker, letting the cold metal dig into my bare shoulder blades. "I've got to find a way to convince her to talk this through and put it behind us. If not, I might as well arrange to break my leg or something because my game is going to be worthless until I get some fucking closure."

"You're a closure-needing person," Brendan agrees, propping a booted foot on top of the bench between us. "But maybe it isn't time for that right now."

I cross my arms at my chest. "What do you mean?"

"Maybe it isn't time to put this behind you. Maybe you need to keep moving forward."

I frown. "What?"

"Keep giving her lessons. Keep going until she's comfortable," Brendan says, like it's the most obvious thing in the world. "I mean, I've never been in your position, but I would think it would pretty hard to teach someone how to be relaxed and confident in bed without actually getting them into bed."

I snort. "Dude, I can't do that. Libby's not that kind of person. She's not going to be on board with becoming fuck buddies." And I'm not sure I'm on board with it, either. Yes, being with Libby this afternoon was hot as hell, but I don't want to hurt her, and I'm not sure she's capable of separating the physical from the emotional or keeping things in the sack "just friendly." Breaking a girl's heart is never fun, but breaking Libby's would haunt me for a damned long time.

"How do you know?" Brendan asks. "You haven't asked her."

"Well, no, but…" I shake my head. "But I know Libby. She likes rules and lists and a place for everything and everything in its place."

"So maybe the reason she was upset this afternoon was because you two hadn't talked about the possibility of hands-on stuff beforehand. Maybe she would be okay with it if you made some rules, set some boundaries."

"I seriously doubt that." But a tiny voice inside me insists that he could have a point. Libby is the kind of person who likes to know what she's getting into.

When we used to go skiing in high school, she would study the map and scope out the harder runs from the green trails before she would even get on a lift. And she's the only person I've ever known who plans out her meals a month in advance to make sure she doesn't end up throwing out leftovers. She's anal-retentive, but in a cute way. And I'm not about to fault her for the food thing.

She spent a month student teaching in Bolivia while she was in college and had to stand in front of a classroom of hungry little kids every day. Since then, she can't throw out so much as half a sleeve of crackers without thinking of those kids and their families, and how grateful they would be for one fifth of what we take for granted.

Libs has reasons for the things she takes seriously. And they aren't always what a person might expect.

So maybe…

"But how can I talk about rules or boundaries if she won't answer the phone?" I cast a glance toward the showers, where most of the team has already finished up. Nowicki will be back any second, and I need to have this heart-to-heart with Brendon finished before he does.

"Stage an intervention," Brendan says with a shrug. "You know her. You can probably figure out where she's going to be tomorrow. When you do, show up and make your pitch in person. Odds are she'll stick around long enough to hear you out, or at least give you the chance to apologize."

I nod, mulling it over. "Yeah. Maybe I will."

"Do it," Brendan says firmly. "You don't give fifty percent on the ice. There's no reason a friend should get fifty percent. If you're going to help Libby, help her. If not, cut your losses and book an appointment with your shrink, ASAP."

"Meditation expert," I correct again as Brendan hitches his bag over his shoulder.

"Whatever you need to tell yourself." He smirks, making it clear he's fucking with me. "Just fix it. None of us want to suffer through another practice like tonight. It was painful to be a part of."

"I know." I run a clawed hand through my sweat-damp hair. "I'll take care of it, captain."

"I'm not here as your captain. I'm here as your friend," he says, his smile fading. "And because life's too short to let good people slip through your fingers. I know Libby's important to you. Don't let one weird afternoon destroy something that's taken years to build. Whether you keep going with the lessons or not, fight for her. Let her know she matters."

"Will do," I say, because he's right. And because I know how personal stuff like this is for him.

He and Maryanne were as close as two people could be, but I know he still feels like there was too much left unsaid between them when she died. That's why he and his little girl, Chloe, text pretty much constantly, even though she's barely seven. He wants his daughter to know that she can talk to him about anything, anytime, anywhere, and he'll always make time to listen.

"Thanks, man," I add as he starts toward the exit, feeling grateful that I have friends who are older and wiser and invested in helping me not fuck up. "I appreciate the advice."

"No problem." Brendan points a finger my way. "But don't tell Laura I thought you two were having a thing, okay?"

"Yeah, and don't tell anyone about…" I trail off as Nowicki emerges from the shower and starts back toward his locker. "About you know who. If we do move forward, it will be on a top-secret basis."

Brendan nods. "Got it." He heads out, leaving me alone with Nowicki, who quickly reminds me why I'm not ready to be the older, wiser person in his life.

"I was thinking in the shower," he says as he pops his locker. "You can't invoke the family rule for people who aren't actually family. So technically, there's no reason I can't ask Libby for her number the next time I see her."

"No reason except that I will beat the ever-loving shit out of you," I say pleasantly. "Don't push me, Nowicki. There are lines that shouldn't be crossed."

I head toward the shower, ignoring Nowicki's laughter and wondering if the line I crossed with Libby is one of those lines, or if there's a chance we can find a way forward as a different sort of friends.

I haven't had a fuck buddy in a long time, but God I would really like to be Libby's. I need the orgasm she deprived me of this afternoon. I need to make her come, to see her cheeks flush pink as she gives in and lets go. I want to get her off with my fingers, to feel her desire wet and sticky on my skin as I take her over the edge. I want my mouth between her legs, licking and sucking and fucking her with my tongue until she explodes. I want to memorize the taste of her, the smell of her, the way her soft curves press against me as she wraps her legs around my hips as I guide my—

"Not now, Cruise," I mutter as I head to the end of the row of shower spigots, talking myself back from a semi. I'm not going to walk around the locker room with a hard-on like a fucking creep.

I'm going to think calm, cool, sexless thoughts until I'm out the door. Then I will go home, soothe my ravaged soul with beer and pizza, and prepare to spend my day off convincing Libby that our lessons don't have to end in disaster.

They can end in satisfaction, pleasure, and more orgasms than she can possibly imagine.

CHAPTER *Eleven*

Libby

From the texts of Justin Cruise and
Libby Collins

Justin: Hey, it's me again. Can we talk today?
Please, Libs, I think we should talk this through,
don't you? We'll both feel better once we clear
the air.

20 minutes later…

Justin: I know you're home, Libby. Laura told me
you skipped your Sunday morning bike ride to
work on your lesson plans.
And no, I didn't tell Laura anything. I was very
subtle while getting my information. Laura has no
clue what's going on, but unfortunately, neither
do I. Like I said yesterday, I'm sorry if I hurt your

feelings or scared you or made you feel like our friendship isn't important to me.

It's very important to me. YOU are very important to me.

So can we please meet up somewhere? Please?

Or at least talk on the phone?

15 minutes later…

Justin: How about texting, then?

Or email?

Morse code?

Smoke signals?

Tell me if I'm getting warmer…

10 minutes later…

Justin: Sorry about that last text. I'm not trying to make a joke of this, I promise. I'm taking this seriously and I feel like shit that I let you down.

I was so pissed at myself that I played like a rookie at practice last night. All I could think about was you and everything that went down and how terrible it felt to be fighting with you, or on your bad side, or whatever is happening right now.

I actually didn't realize you had a bad side. Somehow I've managed to avoid making you angry for over a decade, and I would like to keep avoiding it because you're one of my favorite people and one of my oldest friends and…

Shit, please talk to me, Libby. I'll do anything.
I don't want to lose you…

I stare at the phone as I board the bus headed toward the Hoyt Arboretum, one of my favorite peaceful places in the city. I've been looking forward to a twelve-mile hike through the festival of fall leaves all morning. I got up early to complete my lesson plans for the week and prep for a craft project my kids will be doing on Tuesday so I would have the luxury of staying in the woods as long as I needed in order to find my center.

Instead, my phone keeps reminding me of the man who threw me off said center, the friend who, in one afternoon, rocked me to the core of my being and made me question everything I've ever assumed to be true about myself.

Until yesterday, I'd been sure that I was the type of person who couldn't experience desire without love coming along for the ride. And though I do love Justin, I'm not *in love* with him. He's my goofy, impulsive, comfortable old friend. I would do anything for him, but I don't want to get married and have his babies.

No, I just want to get him naked and ride him the way I did on my couch. Except this time, I don't want either of us to be wearing clothes, and I want that long, thick ridge I felt behind the fly of Justin's jeans to be buried deep inside of me. I want casual sex and more of the incredible, wild, out of control way Jus made me feel, and no amount of thinking about Roger and how perfect we are for each other has been able to put this fire out.

In fact, I spent half the night twisting and turning in bed, tormented by the dirtiest dreams I've had in my entire life.

Dreams in which Justin pinned my wrists to my mattress and whispered filthy things in my ear while he made love to me hard and fast and deep until I came so hard it felt like I would die from the intensity of it all.

But of course, it hadn't been "making love." It had been banging, pure and simple.

And dirty. And hot. So, so hot…

My phone vibrates again, and I look down to see another text—

Justin: What if I wrote you a poem?
Would you talk to me if I wrote you a poem?

I can't help but smile at that one. A poem.

This from the guy I know hasn't read anything besides *Sports Illustrated* and the occasional hockey player autobiography in years. I'm half tempted to text back—*yes, write me a poem, Cruise, and make it rhyme*—just to see what he comes up with, but I'm not ready yet.

I know we have to get past this—Justin and I have too much history to stop talking for a year just because he nearly made me have my first non-self-administered orgasm—but I can't imagine looking him in the eye right now. I would blush so hard I would catch fire, and end up a pile of cinders at his feet. I've never been in a situation like this, and I don't know how to handle it any more than I know how to handle chatting up a stranger on a blind date or casually and organically leaving first base and sliding into second.

You certainly had no trouble yesterday. You were rounding second and heading for third without a hitch.

Heck, if you'd given Justin another half hour, he would have taken care of your virginity problem and you would no longer be in possession of Portland's oldest hymen. Which would probably be great for your self-confidence. Admit it—it would be a lot easier to date without knowing that you're going to have to break the news about your ancient V-card to Mr. New Guy sooner or later.

It would be easier, but the thought of having sex with Justin makes me feel like I've swallowed the entire contents of the arboretum's butterfly garden.

First of all, I've always wanted my first time to be something special and magical, shared with someone I love as more than a friend. Secondly, there's the very real chance that Justin and I won't come out whole on the other side of something like that. I could lose his friendship, and I don't like to think about my life without Jus in it. Not only does he share my geeky love of crafts and make the cutest Christmas ornaments for my tree every year, but he makes me laugh when no one else can. He plays it cool most of the time, but Justin has a soft heart, and he gets me in a way not even Laura or my parents always do.

When a school shooting of innocent babies the same age as my kindergarten kids sent me into a downward spiral of grief and rage a few years ago, Jus was the one who sat with me and let me cry without trying to fix me.

He seemed to realize that I couldn't be fixed, at least not right away. I needed time to grieve the loss of something even bigger than those priceless, precious lives. I needed to grieve the loss of my own innocence, my belief that my country would pull together and do something in the face of such brutal, senseless violence instead of dismissing the tragedy as the cost of doing business in a country more in love with guns than children. Justin gave me that time, and when the moment was right he introduced me to a friend who volunteers for a group working to improve gun safety and helped me get involved.

It's just a single example of the ways in which his friendship has made my world a better place, and I know that I do the same for him. That kind of relationship is priceless and not worth risking for a few orgasms, even if they are as incredible as I imagine they would be.

I'm about to text Justin and tell him that I think it's best if we pretend yesterday never happened—and beg him to give me a few days to recover from my embarrassment before we do our best to return to normal—when my phone vibrates again.

Justin: A Poem for Libby:
If you were a note I'd hold you until I ran out of breath
If you were an addict I'd help you get treatment for meth.
If you were a joke you'd always make me grin, and
If you were a fart I wouldn't hold you in.
(Or maybe I would hold you in, so we could be together and talk through this until we're good again. This is assuming we could talk if you were made of gas and lived in my intestines. Please don't hate me for this terrible poem and disgusting imagery. The end.)

I laugh out loud—loudly out loud—earning myself a curious look from the tweens furiously texting in the seat across from mine. I recognize the "what could someone as old and boring as that lady be laughing about" expression on their faces, and that seals the deal.

I am not old and boring. I'm not even twenty-five! I've got my entire life stretching out in front of me, and I want that life to have fun, sexy, surprising things in it. And that's not going to happen if I keep hiding and running away.

Holding on to the flash of courage, I quickly type—*Headed to the arboretum for a walk. Meet me by the meditation chapel in half an hour?*—and hit send.

A moment later Justin responds with: *Be there in fifteen. Thanks, Libby. See you soon, beautiful.*

Beautiful…

The word makes me wrinkle my nose and sends a fluttery feeling through my midsection at the same time. It reminds me of yesterday, when Justin insisted that I was beautiful, not just pretty. He has never said anything like that before. Part of becoming friends when I was a scrawny thirteen-year-old with braces and he was a drop-dead gorgeous high school sex god is that looks never entered the picture for us.

Yes, I was always aware that Jus was pretty to look at, but I was equally aware that it didn't matter. He was too old, too good-looking, too popular and perfect for me to think of him in that way. Even as we grew older, the mental moat around the idea of Justin as an attractive member of the opposite sex remained. My thoughts didn't even try to cross it. Like I said to myself yesterday—he's a shark and I'm a goldfish. Neither is necessarily better than the other, they simply exist in different worlds, different universes.

But with that one word—*beautiful*—Justin dropped the drawbridge down over the moat, leaving me wondering…

Was yesterday more than an impulsive kiss that

went way too far?

What if Justin has feelings? For me? What the heck am I going to do about it? How am I going to tell one of my best friends, someone I treasure with all my heart, that I don't feel that way about him? That for me, the attraction is purely physical, with no romantic daydreams involved?

For a moment, I consider texting him back and telling him not to come, or jumping off the bus at the next stop and ghosting on him the way I did yesterday, but I force myself stay in my seat.

If Justin has feelings for me, the kindest thing I can do is let him down as swiftly and gently as possible. It's time to put on my big-girl panties and deal with the insanity that my stupid "sex education" plan put in motion, even if it means hurting a person I never, ever want to cause any pain.

CHAPTER
Twelve

Justin

The Hoyt Arboretum is only a few minutes from my apartment. During the summer, I run these trails—through the cool redwoods and up the gorge to the old mill where there are stairs to pound up and down until I'm breathless—at least once or twice a week. Once the season starts, I'm usually too busy to squeeze in another run outside of practice, but damn, have I been missing out.

As I head up the trail toward the meditation chapel, an open A-frame structure made of redwood planks, with a sweet view of the forest rolling down the hill below it, the colors take my breath away. The rest of Portland in the fall isn't anything to turn your nose up at, but the hundreds of rare trees planted and nurtured in this reserve have transformed the forest into something magical. Vivid orange, red, and yellow leaves set the tree tops on fire as they mingle in the canopy. It reminds me of a Chinese New Year celebration, the colors mixing together overhead until they're like silk dragon kites rippling in the breeze.

Fuck, I love fall in this city. I truly am a lucky bastard, to get to play the game I love, in the city I love, and to travel just enough to make me grateful for long weekends at home with friends and family.

Speaking of friends…

I step into the shade under the meditation chapel's roof to see Libby pacing the floor on the other side of the open space. Her side is sunny, and the warm autumn light catches her hair, bringing out streaks of red and gold I hadn't realized were there. She's wearing a dark orange sweater over another pair of baggy linen pants and a hand-knit lacy brown scarf that looks like it was spun by a spider. She's beautiful, in a cozy kind of way, but it isn't an outfit that should give a man an immediate hard-on.

"Get a grip, asshole," I mutter beneath my breath, willing my stupid cock to give it a rest. Yes, cock, I get it, the message has been received. We're attracted to Libby, but that's fucking irrelevant at the moment.

Chances are it will be irrelevant for the foreseeable future, maybe even the rest of our lives. I'm not a mind reader, but Libby certainly doesn't look relaxed and open to continuing what we started She looks stressed, anxious, and when she turns and her eyes meet mine across the shadowy interior of the chapel, a pained expression tightens her features.

"I'm sorry, Libby. I'm an asshole," I say, hating that I'm the one who made her this upset. "Seriously. I'm sorry."

"You don't have to be sorry." Her fingers tangle in her spider-web scarf. "*I'm* sorry. I'm the one who started this, and now things are weird and it's all my fault."

"It's not your fault. It's mine. I shouldn't have kissed you." I close the distance between us, coming to stand beside her in the sun, wishing I could pull her in for a hug and make this better. But I've got an ugly feeling that's it's going to be a long time before hugs between Libby and I are anything but strained and complicated. "At the moment it seemed like a good idea, but clearly it upset you, and it was a bad call and…I'm sorry."

"The kiss isn't what upset me. It was more…" She sighs, glancing away with a shake of her head. "It doesn't matter."

"It does matter." I step closer, unable to resist reaching up to brush her silky hair over her shoulder. "Talk to me, beautiful. Come on, we could always talk. Let's just get it all out, and then we can decide how to move on from wherever we are."

She looks up, focusing on my lips before her

gaze slides up to meet mine, making me keenly aware of how close our mouths are. So close I can smell honey on her breath and feel the warmth of her skin on my face, two relatively innocent things that nevertheless make the hard-on situation worse than it was before.

Christ, I'm fucking hopeless.

"I care about you so much. I hope you know that," Libby says, her words sending a cool sliver of fear cutting through my arousal.

Shit, is Libby about to confess that she has a thing for me? And if so, what the hell am I going to do about it? The last thing I want is to hurt her, but my cock is the only part of me invested in getting her naked. I love her, but I don't love her in that way. She's my sweet friend who I also want to fuck until we're both coming so hard we can't see. That's it.

"You are so important to me," she continues, anxiety tightening the skin around her soft brown eyes. "But yesterday wasn't… I mean it felt amazing, and I've never been so comfortable with someone in a situation like that, but I…"

I frown, confused again. "Just spit it out, Libs."

Her breath rushes out. "I'm not interested in you in that way, Jus. I mean, I'm clearly attracted to you, but you're my friend. And that's all. And I'm sorry if it seemed like I was leading you on with the sex education thing or trying to turn friendship into something more, but I honestly just wanted—"

She keeps talking, but I can't make out what she's saying because I'm laughing too fucking hard. I laugh so hard that after a moment, Libby starts laughing with me.

"What's so funny, jerk?" She shoves my shoulder playfully. "I'm trying to be nice to you so you won't get your feelings hurt!"

"I know. It's nice," I say, fighting to get the words out.

"So, you're not secretly in love with me." She crosses her arms at her chest and glares up at me, but I can tell she's as relieved as I am.

"No, I'm not." I pull in a ragged breath, regaining control. "But I appreciate how sweet you are. Thank you for letting me down easy, babes. You're the best."

She shoves me again, sending another chuckle rumbling through my chest. "And you're the worst. What a jerk you are! You're the one who was calling me beautiful and writing poetry. What was I supposed to think?"

"I get it," I say, laughter fading. "I totally do. For real. I was actually a little worried that you might want something more than friendship."

Her shoulders hunch closer to her ears. "No, I don't. But I am confused. I didn't think I could feel the kind of things I felt yesterday for a friend."

I nod, memories of Libby's expression pre-orgasm making my voice husky when I say,

"Yeah, well, that's why they call it friends with benefits."

"I've never had a friend with benefits." Her gaze drifts to my lips again, making me think I'm not the only one with sex on the brain.

"I have. It can be nice, as long as both people are on the same page emotionally." I shift closer, pulling the heavenly smell of her in along with my next breath. "Which, it seems like we are…"

Her chest rises and falls, her heart-stopping breasts straining the fabric of her sweater, making me ache to set them free. "This is not something I've even considered until today, Jus. I've always been a romantic, but…" She looks up, heat and uncertainty mixing in her eyes. "But I don't want to be a disaster in the bedroom for the rest of my life. And I'm not sure I'm going to learn what I want to learn any other way."

"You're not a disaster," I promise. "I meant what I said yesterday, Libs. I wanted you. So fucking much. You made me crazy."

"And then I ran away." Her teeth trap her bottom lip for a moment before setting it free, making me remember how good it felt to have those teeth raking over my skin. "Because I'm a stress case. But I don't want to be anymore. I want to be confident and sure of myself and know that I can *you-know-what* with another person in the room and the world isn't going to come to an end."

"You know what?"

"That I can come," she whispers, her cheeks going pink.

My eyebrows lift sharply. "You've never…"

She shakes her head as her gaze drops to where her fingers tangle in her scarf. "No. Brett tried and tried, but it never happened. It got to be such an insurmountable, stressful obstacle that I would just fake it. It was easier than dealing with a frustrated boyfriend and feeling like a failure every time we were together. And with the other men I've dated, things never went that far."

"Shit," I mutter, the knowledge that she's been deprived of lover-administered orgasms—and that Brett is probably the only man she's ever slept with—penetrating the lust fog building between us.

This is a bigger responsibility than I thought. But hell, knowing I'm going to be the first man to make Libby come makes me want to take her right here, to pull her into the shadows beneath the chapel ceiling beams and get her off.

She laughs softly, her eyes glittering. "No, Justin."

"No, what?" I move in as she backs a step away.

"I'm not the only one whose face gives her away," she says, lifting her palms in front of her with another giggle. "No! We're not jumping into anything, especially in the middle of a public park. We need to talk, set some ground rules."

"Ground rule number one—I make you come

at least once a day every day that I'm in town for the next month." I continue to stalk her across the chapel as she retreats with an intrigued expression that makes me hope she's going to let me catch her. "Then we touch base over Thanksgiving and decide if we want to keep taking our clothes off or go back to being friends without orgasms. Done. Rules complete."

"No, not done," she insists. "Ground rule number two—we keep this a secret from everyone else, especially friends and family."

"Ground rule number three—you have to be honest with me, no faking."

"And you have to be honest with me." She comes to a stop, her back against one of the support beams. "If I suck at this you have to tell me. I don't want your pity. I want to make you feel the way that you make me feel."

"And how's that?"

She holds my gaze, the heat in her eyes making my cock swell thicker. "Good. Very, very good."

"I haven't made you feel good yet." I brace my hands on either side of her flushed face. "But I want to, Libs." I bend closer, loving the way her breath catches as my nose brushes against hers. "Let me make you come, beautiful. I need to touch you, and I'm fucking dying to kiss you again."

"But what if someone comes up the trail?" she says, but her resolve is weakening, I hear it in her voice.

"Then we'll stop," I promise, wrapping an arm around her waist and pulling her tight against me. Her soft moan as my erection comes in contact with the soft curve of her belly is all the encouragement I need to bring my other hand to her breast, cupping her through the soft weave of her sweater, teasing her tight nipple. "Come on, Libs. Let me show you how good it feels to lose control."

"Ground rule number four," she whispers as her arms come around my neck. "We keep things equal."

"Which means?" I pinch her nipple lightly, making her moan again, a sweet, soft sound I'm already positive I'll never get tired of hearing.

"If you make me come, then I intend to return the favor." She reaches down, dragging her nails lightly over my erection through my jeans and the last of my control vanishes.

A moment later, I've got Libby's legs looped around my waist as I pin her to the massive redwood beam and kiss her so hard and deep I hope there's no doubt in her mind how sexy she is. How hot. So hot that I can't wait to get her home tonight, where I can strip her bare and fuck her the way she deserves to be fucked. I'm going to take her slow and steady and so thoroughly that by the time I'm finished there will be nothing left but a puddle of boneless, orgasm-drunk Libby lying limp and supremely satisfied in my bed.

For now, I'll have to be satisfied with something a little faster, but I still intend to rock her fucking world.

CHAPTER
Thirteen

Libby

Oh my God, oh my God. Oh yes, oh my God…
As Justin kisses me like he's going to devour me whole, and his hand slips beneath my sweater, my thoughts are an endless, blissed out stream of nonsense. I can't think, I can only feel, feel, *feel* all the electric, intense, incredible things he makes me feel. With just a single kiss, a touch, the warmth of his body and the strength in his arms as he effortlessly holds me in the air with one arm and teases my nipples with the other, I'm completely under his command.

He takes control, leaving no room for anxiety or fear or worry about what comes next or the fact that we might be discovered. My world narrows to his taste, his heat, his mouth, and his hands working magic across my skin.

"You're coming home with me after this." His

breath is hot on my throat as he kisses me there, sending fresh butterflies swooping through my belly. "And then I'm going to take off your sweater and your bra, and I'm going to show you what I can do to this sweet little nipple with my mouth."

"Oh God," I murmur, because that is the extent of my vocabulary at this moment, as he lays me down on the cool concrete and covers me with his body, his fingers already working open the string tie at the top of my pants.

"Is the ground too hard?" His voice is as soft as the fingers he brushes back and forth beneath the elastic of my panties.

"No," I whisper, clinging to his shoulders, ignoring the prickle of fear creeping in at the back of my thoughts. "But it's hard to pay attention to anything but how much I want you to touch me."

"I can't wait to touch you." His hand eases lower, making my pulse spike as he reaches the curls between my legs. "Spread your legs for me, Libby. Let me make you wet, beautiful."

Holding my breath, I force my thighs to relax, fully anticipating at least a beat or two of awkwardness as I adjust to the reality that Justin is touching me where only one man has ever touched me before. But then his fingertips brush over my clit, sending a bolt of electricity sweeping through me so sharp and sweet that I'm still reeling from the intensity of it when he finds my entrance and pushes inside.

I moan again as his finger glides deeper, making me aware of every nerve ending in my inner walls. They are all firing and pulsing, awake and alive in a way they've never been before.

"Fuck, you're tight, Libs," Justin groans as he kisses me again, the magic of his tongue in my mouth and his hand between my legs making me feel like I'm caught in a riptide, helpless to resist being pulled out to sea. "And so wet. God, I love feeling how wet you are, baby, how much you want me."

"Yes," I sigh in agreement, sliding my palm down his erection, breath rushing out against his lips as his cock pulses beneath my touch. I love feeling how much he wants me, too. I love it so much that I suddenly can't wait to feel the hard, hot length of him in my hand.

I tug at the top of his jeans, popping the button and dragging down the zipper. His groan of pleasure as I slip my fingers beneath the waist of his boxers and wrap my fingers around his erection is almost enough to banish the flash of concern as I realize how large he is.

Almost…

Geez Louise-us. I'm not sure yet how long he is, but his girth alone is terrifying. As I stroke him up and down, I can't quite get my fingertips to meet around his thickness. Even if we decide full-fledged sex is something we're both on board with, I'm not sure he'll fit.

We may be more like a shark and a goldfish

than I ever imagined, in that his giant shark cock will never ever fit inside my goldfish-size vagina.

I'm imagining the devastation that would be left behind—the vaginal equivalent of a tornado ripping through a trailer park, leaving death and destruction in its wake—when Justin's thumb starts to circle my clit and I'm swept back into the riptide of pleasure.

"You can hold me tighter, Libs," Jus murmurs against my lips between kisses. "I'm not going to break." I adjust my grip, a powerful thrill rushing through me as he gasps, "Fuck, yes. Just like that, Libby. God, that feels so good," and thrusts into the fingers I've fisted around his cock.

I'm doing it right! Now if I can manage to keep doing it right as Justin drives me completely out of my mind…

The combination of his thumb on my clit and his fingers—two of them now, filling me until I'm blissfully, perfectly full—are quickly taking me back to that wild, wind-swept place where there is nothing to hold on to, nothing but pleasure and tension and the white-hot rush of my blood thundering through my veins as I lean into the abyss.

"Yes, baby." Justin rakes his teeth across the skin at my throat. "Oh fuck, yes, Libby, come for me."

"I'm close," I gasp. God, I'm so close…

"Come for me, beautiful. Let me feel you."

So close…

"Fuck, Libby, I'm almost there. I'm almost—"

I call his name as my release crashes over me, making it feel like a nuclear bomb has been detonated in my core. The pleasure is fierce, merciless, wringing through me in powerful waves as Justin's hand continues to move between my legs, drawing the orgasm out into a long, lovely, in-freaking-credible thread of beauty that is as close to heaven as I've ever been.

It is mind-blowing, life-changing, world-view-altering in ways that I can't process right away. All I know, as I lie there beneath Justin, catching my breath, is that my vibrator is no match for this man.

Not even close.

"Wow," he says, his breath warm on my lips. "I swear it usually takes me longer than that. I guess I was more worried about getting caught that I thought."

I glance down, realizing that the top of my hand and my wrist are covered in milky-white stickiness, and another unfamiliar wave of satisfaction and pride washes through me. Well, unfamiliar in a sexual situation, anyway. I was so lost in my own release I missed Justin's. But he came. I made him come, *made* this drop-dead sexy man who's probably seen more action in the bedroom in the past month than I've seen in my entire life lose control.

"I want to watch you next time." The words are out of my mouth before I can worry about whether they're the right thing to say, another unusual-for-the-bedroom occurrence.

But then, we're not in a bedroom. We're in the middle of a public park, where we could be discovered at any moment. And I'm still lying here with Justin's hand on my stomach and his release all over my hand.

"Watch me come?" He pulls back, that sexy, simmering look in his eyes again. When I nod, he adds in a husky voice, "I think that can be arranged. Let's go back to my place. I'll make you come on my mouth until you beg for mercy, and then you can return the favor, if you're up for it."

"Yes," I say, giddy at the thought. "But you'll have to teach me how. I've only done that once and I was really bad at it."

"I seriously doubt that, Libs." He cleans my hand with the bottom of his tee shirt before tucking himself back in his jeans. "Have you ever thought that maybe it wasn't you who was the problem, babes? I mean, Brett became a priest, for God's sake."

"Literally." I giggle at my joke, smile widening when Justin laughs with me.

"Right." He sits up beside me as I pull my clothes back into place. "He was probably dealing with a lot of guilt about sex, and guilt makes everything un-fun and un-sexy. Even with a smoking-hot fox like you."

I sit up, crossing my legs. "I don't feel guilty now. Do you?"

"Not even a little bit." His gaze burns into mine with a heat that gives me a full body shiver. "I can't wait to show you all the different ways I can make you come. It's my new fucking mission in life, Libs. Literally."

I grin and lean in, giving him an impulsive kiss that turns into something slow and sweet and oh so good.

When we finally part, I'm warm and tingling all over, and so grateful to Jus for what he's done for me already that I decide not to worry about the monster in his pants. When and *if* we decide to go that far, I can talk to him about my concerns and we'll work through it together. Jus is my friend, and has been for years, and he's right, we've always been able to talk.

It might be a little awkward, but I can talk to him about anything, even the possibility that he might have elephantiasis of the penis.

I snort, but cover it with a cough as Jus helps me to my feet.

"What's so funny?" he asks, eyes narrowed.

I shake my head. "Nothing. I'm just happy. Thank you."

"You don't have to thank me. Seriously, Libby, I'm going to get every bit as much out of this as you are. Now I don't have to worry about rebounding from Sylvia, and I'll get to spend some quality time with a very good friend. Naked. Have I mentioned that I'm really excited about getting you naked?"

I bite my lip, fighting a smile. "I'm pretty excited about getting you naked, too. You're not the most hideous specimen I've seen, Cruise."

"You either, Collins." He chuckles as he loops an arm around my shoulders, hugging me close as we start back through the chapel toward the trail. "But can we stop for pizza on the way back to my place? I skipped lunch and I'm going to need something to keep my stamina up until one or two in the morning."

"I have to be at school by seven a.m.," I warn him. "Some of us work normal hours for a living, you know."

"Does that mean you're not sleeping over?" He sounds so sad I can't help but laugh.

"No, it means, we're asleep by ten, so I can get up at six and swing by my place to shower and change clothes before I head into school. Or we could just go to my place instead…"

He shakes his head. "No, my place is closer, and I have a Jacuzzi. And I need to do terrible wonderful things to you in there as soon as possible."

"Okay." I glance up at him, my stomach fluttering. "Just don't move too fast, okay? Maybe take the training wheels off a little at a time?"

"Don't worry, Libs," he says, expression sobering. "I get it. There's no pressure on my end. Like I said, I just want to make you feel good. We'll go slow, you can ask all the questions you want, and we'll keep the lines of communication open. If I'm doing something you don't like, or vice versa, we'll talk about it, make adjustments, and we'll both come hard and often. It's all good."

"Sounds good," I say, cheeks heating again. "And maybe I'll eventually stop blushing every time we have a conversation like this."

He shrugs. "Or keep blushing. You're cute when you blush. And you're stunning when you come. Seriously, so far I can't see that you have anything to be insecure about. You're beautiful, babes, and so fucking sexy."

This time the heat doesn't stop at my cheeks. It radiates throughout my entire body, making me feel like I'm glowing. But it's a happy glow, a hopeful glow, and walking through the woods with Justin's arm around me and my hand still a little sticky feels good.

Hell, better than good. This might be one of the best days of my life, and I get to share it with someone I love, even if it's not in *that* way. I'm a lucky woman.

And I'm about to get even luckier…

CHAPTER
Fourteen

Justin

We grab a pie from Papa Mack's and are back on the road in just a few minutes. All the way back to my place, I keep my hand on Libby's thigh, my thoughts a non-stop smut-fest, featuring all the things I'm going to do to her as soon as I get her alone. First on my couch, then in my bed, and then in my Jacuzzi with my hands soaping her breasts while I reveal to her why my magic jets are so magical.

The thought of making her come, again and again, until she's completely wasted on orgasms is enough to keep me rock-hard and aching, even before I allow myself to imagine her lips parting around my cock, her pink tongue circling the tip as I show her just how easy it is to make a man lose his fucking mind.

Two days ago, the thought of pumping

between Libby's lips while she sucked me off would have given me a guilt complex, but now it's right up there with the most anticipated events of my year, right along with setting a scoring record for the Badgers and taking my boat on a cruise down the coast to Mexico as soon as the season is through.

"What are you thinking?" Libby asks, as we stop at a light not far from my place, waiting for the damned thing to turn green. Of course we're hitting every damned light. It's like the universe can sense how desperate I am to get Libs alone and is doing everything in its power to prolong the sweet torture.

"I'm thinking about your pussy," I answer honestly. "And how I can't wait to make you come all over my face."

She laughs—soft and surprised—and her thighs squeeze closer together, trapping my hand between them. "You have the filthiest mouth."

"That's not filthy. It would be filthy if I said I can't wait to fuck your sweet cunt with my tongue," I say, curling my fingers into her muscled flesh. "That I can't wait to be drowning in you because I've made you come so hard. Or if I said I'm dying to have your tits in my mouth while I—"

"Okay," she says with another breathy laugh. "Point taken."

"Not a fan of dirty talk? If so, I can tone it down." *At least until we're naked and you're riding my cock and I lose all control over the words coming out of my mouth.* I know myself too well to think I'll be able to Boy Scout it up that much. "Like I said, I want us to be honest with each other, Libs. If the dirty stuff turns you off, I want to know."

"No, I…" She clears her throat. "No, it's okay."

"Okay?" I repeat incredulously. "Okay like oatmeal is okay for breakfast? Okay like soap is an okay gift if you haven't known someone for very long. Okay like—"

"No, okay as in you're cleared for dirty talk," she says, a naughty grin curving her lips. "I like it."

"Yeah? How much do you like it?" My cock shoves against my zipper, insisting it's going to fall off of my body as an act of protest if I don't get out of these jeans in the next ten minutes.

Damn traffic light. If we were at the front of the line, I would run it.

Libby turns my way, meeting my gaze as she says in a soft voice, "Well, my panties are wet again. So I'd say that's a pretty good sign."

I curse beneath my breath. "Oh, sweet Libs, I'm going to make a dirty girl of you yet, and it's going to be a beautiful, beautiful thing."

She smiles, her dimple popping. "You should drive," she says, just as the guy behind me lays on the horn.

I put the pedal to the metal, making it to the parking garage in record time and swinging into my space fast enough to make the tires squeal. The second I shove the car into park and cut the engine, I lean over, capturing Libby's mouth for a kiss, groaning as her tongue dances and swirls against mine, her shyness clearly a thing of the past. I can feel her hunger in the way her fingers dig into my shoulders, in the way she angles her head, granting me even deeper access to her sweet mouth.

And then she reaches down to caress the bulge in my jeans through the strained fabric, and for a moment I go blind with wanting her.

"Upstairs," I order against her lips. "Now. And the second we're through the door I want your clothes off, Libby."

"Filthy and bossy," she says, her words turning to a gasp as I cup her pussy possessively, rubbing the heel of my hand against her clit.

"Yes, I am bossy, but you like it. I can tell." I rest my forehead against hers as I continue to tease her through her pants, making her breath come faster. "And you're going to like it even more as soon as I get you out of these clothes. I fucking promise you that, Libs. So, what are you going to do as soon as we get to my place, beautiful?"

"I'm going to take off my clothes." She pulses into my hand with a moan.

"And what else are you going to do?"

"Whatever you tell me to do," she says, sending another bolt of need straight to my already aching balls. "Within reason."

"Good girl," I say, feeling pretty sure I can make her forget about reason. If I can't, I don't deserve to be the man at the helm of her sex education.

But I know I do. And I know I can. All I need is time, four walls, and a lock I can turn to make sure Libby and I aren't disturbed until I've shown her how much she's been missing.

We hurry out of the car, forgetting the pizza in the back seat in our dash for the elevator. I sprint back for it—we're going to need sustenance to keep our energy up for coming our brains out—and rejoin Libby as the elevator dings open and we make out all the way up to the twelfth floor. I've got a beautiful woman in one arm and a pizza balanced on the other, and I'm positive this is going to be one of the best evenings I've had in a while.

Near the end, Sylvia and I were fighting so often that I haven't had a hot, uncomplicated screw in longer than I would like to admit. And there is something so fucking sexy about Libby right now.

I don't know if it's her relative inexperience that has me so turned on—there's little I enjoy more than teaching someone I love a pastime I love—or her curvy little body, or something chemical that's flipped a switch in my brain, but I'm out of my goddamned mind with lust. I'm so focused on getting Libby inside and under me that at first I don't understand why she grinds to a halt beside me outside the elevator.

"What's—"

"Get down," she hisses, pulling me down to the ground behind the potted plants that frame the elevator door. "Laura's down the hall!"

I curse, breath rushing out as I realize my mistake. "She's coming over to watch movies. I totally fucking forgot."

"How could you forget?" Libby whispers, eyes wide as she watches her sister sashay toward my front door. "Keeping Laura in the dark is at least two of the rules! Your rules, I remind you."

"Sorry. I was distracted by your lips and your breasts and all the other sexy parts of you I'm going to get my mouth on as soon as we get rid of your sister. We'll tell her you're helping me with a crochet project and pick out something insanely hard. In ten minutes she'll be so bored, she'll show herself out."

Libby shakes her head. "No way, Justin. We can't show up together like this. Laura will know something's up the second she looks at my face."

"No, she won't." I sigh again as Libby shoots me a look that encourages me to get fucking real. "Okay, fine. You're right. You look like you can't wait to get me naked and lick me up and down like an ice cream cone."

Her lips quirk. "I was thinking a lollipop, but you're on the right track. Which means I have to make a break for it, and you have to stay here and keep Laura from getting suspicious."

"No way. We'll just head over to your place." I reach up, pressing the down button on the elevator. "I'll call and make my excuses to Laura on the way."

"You can't cancel. You know how she is. If you cancel, she'll take it personally and you'll have to spend a month trying to get back in her good graces."

"I'm okay with that." I jab the down button again.

"Well, I'm not." Her lips are set in a firm line that makes it clear she's well and truly made up her mind. "I don't want whatever we're doing to interfere with your relationship with my sister. I'm calling a car to take me home. All the parts of me that you want to get your mouth on will still be here tomorrow night."

"I have a game tomorrow night. In Seattle."

"Tuesday night, then," she says.

I wince, the knowledge that I have to wait another forty-eight hours to get more of Libby physically painful. "You promise? Tuesday night you're all mine?"

"I promise," she says, kissing me on the cheek as the elevator doors open. "And I promise you're not going to die."

"If I do, I'm blaming you. I want 'pussy deprivation' etched into my headstone, Collins. And I want you to leave orchids or some other pussy-resembling flower on my grave daily as a gesture of penance. Seriously."

She laughs, kisses me again—this time on the mouth, a quick good-bye peck that leaves me aching for more—before crawling into the elevator on her hands and knees and tapping the ground floor button. "See you Tuesday." Her fingers flutter, the doors slide shut, and she's gone.

With a sigh, I stand, pizza in hand, and think about my shitty practice yesterday. I think about abandoned puppies, people who enjoy Phil Collins music, gummy candies with pockets of liquid inside, and other disgusting and disturbing things, doing my best to get my hard-on under control as I start down the hall, feeling frustrated, thwarted, and miserable. If only I hadn't been so fixated on the erotic benefits of the goddamned Jacuzzi, Libby and I would have ended up at her place and I could be making her come right now.

Fuck!

I love Laura, she is my dear friend, but right now I would like for her to develop a disease that would send her home to bed for the night. Nothing too awful, of course, just enough to keep her out of my hair for the next eight to twelve hours while I do wicked, wonderful things to her little sister.

The little sister she is insanely protective of, and who she would probably beat me into a bloody pulp for introducing to the fuck buddy lifestyle.

The thought is enough to take the edge off, and by the time I round the corner to find Laura outside my door, scrolling through something on her phone, the pity party in my pants has subsided.

"Hey, I was just texting you." She grins as she spots the pizza. "Bless you, you sweet, wonderful man. I've been jonesing for cheese all day long. You're the very best."

"I aim to please," I say, guilt lifting its grubby head inside of me. I am not the very best. I am the jerk who forgot we were meeting up tonight and almost did obscene things to her innocent sister in my bathtub.

Laura leans in for a hug, but pauses before her arms are all the way around my waist. "Where were you just now?"

"What? Why?" I ask, wondering if I've got lipstick on my face or some other telltale sign that might give my near-tryst with Libby away.

"You smell funny," Laura says, her eyes narrowing.

I laugh tightly as I dig into my pocket for my keys. "Thanks, Laura."

"Not in a bad way, just different. But sort of familiar." She leans in, sniffing my shoulder as I open the door, making sweat break out beneath my button-up. "Like flowers or—"

"I stopped in a flower shop to get something to send to Sylvia," I lie. "She wasn't happy about me having all her shit delivered to her office by messenger yesterday, so I figured I should try to make amends. No reason to get on her bad side just because we broke up."

Laura chuckles. "It's cute how you think you're going to stay friends with your exes even though that never ever happens."

"People stay friends with their exes."

"People do, but *you* don't. Name one woman you've previously dated who doesn't run the other way the second she sees your pretty face," Laura says, grunting smugly as I search my memory banks and come up empty. "See. You can't be friends. Once you love 'em and leave 'em you might as well give up, Cruise. You're too much of a heartbreaker to end up on the 'still friends' list."

I open the door, frowning as I hold it for Laura. "But I'm not an asshole about breaking up. At least not all the time, or even most of the time."

"Of course you aren't." Laura pats my chest as she breezes inside and slips out of her coat. "You're just an intense experience for women, I think. Like dry red wine. You either love it or you hate it." She hangs her coat on the antique hooks my interior decorator scattered all over the wall inside the door and turns back to me with a finger held up in the air. "No, you're like vodka. Once you puke it up, you never want to drink it again. You don't even want to think about vodka or look at it or remember that vodka exists."

131

"You were super hungover yesterday, I'm assuming," I say, ready to change the subject.

"So fucking hungover. It was miserable," Laura groans, looping her purse handle over another hook and pulling out a small stack of DVDs. "I hit the dispenser outside of the drugstore and got all the new releases. You want some edgy horror that's supposed to be great, sappy romance with a cheesy-looking dog in it, or some lame science fiction with a thin premise and people wearing too much green makeup?"

"I'm guessing horror, since you made the other two sound so appealing."

"Wise man," Laura says as she heads for the couch. "I would like three slices of whatever that is, please and thank you."

I set the pizza down on the kitchen island and stare out the floor-to-ceiling windows on the other side of my condo at the view of downtown and the mountains beyond, where dark storm clouds are rolling in to darken the bright autumn afternoon.

Laura is right. None of my exes ever want to be friends, and that includes my old fuck buddy Kirsten, who, after finding her true love, George, decided she never wanted to see me again. I was not invited to the wedding, even though Kirsten and I worked at hockey camps together every winter growing up and were seriously tight all through college. And now when we run into each other at the parties of mutual friends, she just nods politely before finding someone else to talk to.

As I fetch plates from the cabinet and grab a roll of napkins, I can't help getting a little freaked out. I don't want Libby to become one of the women who can't stand to look at my face. I don't want to lose her friendship, but I don't want to live the rest of my life without knowing what it feels like to fuck her, either. I want to pleasure her in all the ways I had planned and all the new ones I'll come up with between now and Tuesday night. I want to make her come, make her lose control, make sure she knows what it feels like to be completely erotically satisfied so that she never settles for another dud like Brett again.

But do I want it bad enough to risk never seeing her smile again? To risk having Libby's eyes go cold every time her path crosses mine, which, considering our parents still live next door to each other and her sister works for my team, would be pretty fucking often?

I don't know. I seriously don't.

Even after half a pizza and two movies—the horror and the sci-fi, which is as stupid as Laura suspected it would be—I'm still not sure. All I know is that I have some serious thinking to do. But hopefully I'll be able to confine my thinking to the flight to Seattle. I've got to keep all non-game-related thoughts off the ice, or it's back to five a.m. meditation sessions for me, and I really prefer to sleep a little later than the ass crack of dawn.

"Want to start the romance?" Laura yawns as she stretches her socked feet out onto the leather footstool/coffee table.

"Nah, you're right; the dog looks cheesy."

"So cheesy. And I usually love dog movies, but seriously, pick a breed that doesn't have a permanent grin on its face. I like my dog heroes to be able to project pathos, as well as happy-go-luckiness."

"I'm all about the pathos," I agree.

She snorts. "Do you even know what that means?"

"A quality that inspires sadness, pity, or despair," I answer, clicking off the television and rising to my feet. "I'm not dumb, Laura."

"I know you're not," she says. "Forgive me, I've been spending too much time with your less intelligent teammates. And of course Brendan, who refuses to speak in complete sentences with fans unless I stab him repeatedly with a fork. I feel for him, I really do, and I know he's under a lot of stress as a single dad, but would it kill him to get friendly at promo ops once in a while?"

"Maybe. You never know what straw is going to break a man's back."

Laura hums beneath her breath as she rocks to her feet and starts for the door. "True. I'll try to remember that the next time I ask him to smile for the camera and he glares at me like I stole his

Bible and violated his sister."

I grunt. "I think his sisters all live in Canada, which would make that difficult, but you're funny."

"I know. See you Saturday after the home game? I'm trying to get Libby to come out and play. If she doesn't hook up with a hot tech billionaire, maybe the three of us could go grab ice cream or something?"

"Sure." I'm grateful for the darkness in the entryway so Laura can't see the scowl bunching my forehead. Libby and a hot tech billionaire? What the fuck is that about? "So Libby's going on a blind date?"

"Nah, I'm arranging to have a few eligible bachelors thrown in her path so she can see what's out there. She needs to start dating again. I know she's got her heart set on this guy she works with, but if he's too dumb to see how adorable Libby is, then she should move the hell on."

"Agreed," I say, giving Laura a good-bye hug and telling her, "Drive safe."

When she's gone, I start to text Libby, but then realize it's too late and she'll already be sleeping, and put my phone down. I try to convince myself to hit the sack early, too, but instead I end up back on the couch, watching the sappy romance and trying not to stress about Libby and I ending up on bad terms. Thankfully, the dog isn't as bad as Laura and I thought it would be. The romance isn't half bad, either. I'm not usually a fan, but tonight, love entertains, and by the time I head to bed I'm nearly too tired to jerk off.

Nearly.

But I manage to work up the energy to tug one out to mental images of Libby riding my cock, her hands braced on my chest and her breasts bouncing fetchingly each time she slams home. It's not nearly as good as coming in Libby's hand this afternoon, but it's enough to send me off to sleep, where I dream of Libby under the mistletoe at a holiday party, kissing a man in glasses who isn't me, and refusing to so much as glance my way.

CHAPTER
Fifteen

From the texts of Libby Collins
and Justin Cruise

Libby: Are you in Seattle yet?

Justin: Yeah, we just landed a few minutes ago. We're waiting on the bus to the arena. What's up?

Libby: Nothing. I just wanted to wish you good luck. I know you had a bad practice the other day, and sometimes things like that get under your skin. But there's no need to get weird or superstitious or start thinking the rest of your career is going to suck or that you'll be mocked for the rest of your life for having the worst scoring drought in NHL history.

Justin: This isn't making me feel better, Libby.

Libby: Well, it should. I have complete faith in you.
You're going to have an amazing game. There's no doubt in my mind.

Justin: And what if I don't? What if I miss every pass and fuck up every shot?

Libby: Then you'll do better next time.
Either way, I'm still going to do naughty things to you tomorrow night.

Justin: Oh yeah? Want to describe some of them to me?

Libby: LOL. Are you trying to get me to sext with you?

Justin: It would help quiet my nerves so I can score goals, and I know you want me to score goals, don't you, Libs?
Lots and lots of goals…

Libby: You wanted that to sound dirty, didn't you?

Justin: Absolutely.
Now sext me, Collins. Use those sweet fingers to tell me all the wicked things you're going to do to my body tomorrow night.

Libby: Well, I'm going to get you naked…

Justin: Yes?

Libby: And I'm going to get serious…

Justin: Yes?

Libby: And then I'm…
I'm probably gonna…
Ugh! I don't know how to do this! I've never sexted before!

Justin: YOU'VE NEVER SEXTED BEFORE?

Libby: NO, I HAVEN'T! DON'T MAKE FUN OF ME!

Justin: I'm not. LOL.

Libby: And don't laugh! I'm fully capable of sexting with the best of them, buddy.
You just caught me off guard. But by the time you finish the game tonight, I will have written you lots of excellent sexts. You just wait.

Justin: I look forward to reading them.
And I can't wait for tomorrow, beautiful.

Libby: Me either…
I dreamt about you last night.

Justin: Good dreams, I hope.

Libby: Filthy dreams. I'm going to use them as inspiration for my sexts.
Get ready to have your mind—and your dick—blown, Cruise.

Justin: I'm hard just thinking about it.

Libby: Good. That's the way I like you.

Justin: Nice sass level, Libs.

Libby: Thanks! I told you I'm going to be good at this. I minored in English Lit, man. Me and words on paper—or on a screen—are all good. So please have an amazing game and return to your phone refreshed and ready to fully appreciate my dirty brilliance.

Justin: Will do. And thanks for texting. I appreciate the vote of confidence.

Libby: Of course! That's what friends are for.
I'm always here for you, and being friends with benefits for a little while isn't going to change that.

Justin: That's really good to hear, babes.
And you don't give yourself enough credit, you know. As far as I'm concerned you always know

the right thing to say.

Libby: Well, it's easy with friends. Especially good ones.
Now go kick some Canuck ass.

Justin: Will do.

CHAPTER Sixteen

Justin

I have a new good luck charm, and her name is Libby "The Sexting Goddess" Collins.

After our pre-game texting, I scored on my first shift of the game, slamming the puck into the vulnerable, quivering Canuck net within seconds of hitting the ice. I followed up with an assist in the first period and another goal in the second. Then, during a scrum in the third period, I managed to gouge the Canadian motherfucker who nearly broke my arm last year in the gut without getting caught—because Scorpios never forget, asshole; remember that the next time you think it's a good idea to slam your stick repeatedly into someone's radius.

All in all, it is a glorious fucking game, and I skate off the ice feeling fine.

And then Libby's texts get me feeling even

finer.

Text from Libby: In my dream, I woke up in the middle of the night and the shower was on in the master bathroom. At first I was scared, but then I remembered that you were sleeping over, and I decided that I needed to touch you again.

Immediately.

So I crawled out of bed, stripping off my nightgown as I tiptoed to the bathroom door then eased inside as quietly as I could. I wanted to surprise you, but you turned around as I crossed to the shower.

The moment you saw me through the glass, you started to get hard. You dropped your hand, touching yourself, stroking up and down while you watched me open the door and step into the spray. We smiled, but neither of us said a word. We didn't have to, because we both knew what we wanted. So I dropped to my knees in front of you and you pushed inside my lips, over my tongue, while I sucked you deeper inside my mouth.

And in my dream, you tasted so good, and I knew exactly what to do to make you come so hard you could barely stand when you were finished.

Can't wait to see if reality mirrors fantasy…

Have a safe trip home tomorrow, and here's a little something to keep you company tonight.

At the bottom of the string of sexy-as-fuck texts is a picture of Libby's hips and thighs, her skin bare except for a pair of black lace panties.

They are relatively modest, covering more of her than most two-piece swimsuits, but it doesn't matter. Knowing her sweet pussy is beneath that lace is enough to get my blood pumping nearly as fast as it was out on the ice.

Back at my lonely hotel room, I read over the red-hot lines at least a dozen times and am finally forced to jerk off, yet again—apparently I've reverted to my fifteen-year-old self—to a fantasy involving me returning Libby's oral favor to convince my buzzing brain to go to sleep.

Due to the late hour, I can't text her back immediately, but as soon I wake up, I brew a tiny hotel-room-size pot of coffee and sit down to craft something appropriately filthy in response.

Thankfully, however, I have the sense to remember where Libby works before I hit send.

Sexting and elementary schools do *not* mix. Libby's probably up to her elbows in markers and glue, or helping a small person learn the alphabet. The last thing she needs is a raunchy text about how many times I'm going to make her come tonight popping up on her phone while she's reading *The Day the Crayons Quit*. (Great book. Libby suggested I give a copy to Brendan's art-loving daughter, Chloe, for Christmas last year, and it's still her favorite bedtime story.)

Exercising incredible restraint, I refrain from

responding until exactly three o'clock, when I'm back home and I know Libby's kids have all boarded the bus and the woman herself will be alone in her classroom, tidying up before she heads home for the day.

Then, and only then, do I shoot off my response,

Text from Justin: Dear Sexting Goddess, let's talk about those lace panties and how much I want to rip them off of you. Your texts were hot as fuck, Libs. All I could think about after the game was how much I needed to touch you, taste you, and show you how much I appreciate your filthy mind by eating your pussy for at least a solid hour.

Please arrange to be wearing as little as possible when I get to your place.

See you—and your pussy—around four?

I wait a few moments, hoping she'll text back right away, but my phone remains quiet. She must be in a meeting or something.

Tossing my cell on my bed, I jump into the shower even though I took one at the hotel this morning. I am not an overly stinky man-beast—though you don't want to get anywhere near my skates after a game—but I want to smell soapy and clean for Libby. At least until I find out if she's as much of a freak for a little stink as I am.

I scrub the grundle until it's gleaming like the

softly wrinkled skin of a freshly washed baby elephant, complete my manscaping so that the stick and pucks are presented to their best advantage, and dress in soft jeans and a softer flannel in order to be tactilely pleasing if Libby ends up undressed while I'm still clothed. It's easier to resist the temptation to move too fast when wearing pants, and I don't want to rush a minute with Libby tonight.

I want to take my time, savoring each step on the road to discovering everything that makes her curvy little body hum.

Half an hour later, I'm clean, coiffed, shaved, and ready to roll, but Libby still hasn't responded to my text. I'm about to shoot her another message, when my phone rings.

A smile curving my lips, I answer with a husky, "Hello, sexy. Are you home and naked yet?"

I'm answered by a sniffing sound. "No, I'm not. I'm driving and trying not to cry. I totally screwed it up, Justin."

"Screwed what up?"

"Everything. After last night and the other day in the park, I was feeling so confident in my not-repulsiveness that I decided to ask Roger what he was doing on Saturday. To see if he wanted to come to the game with me. You know, just as friends or whatever."

"Okay," I say, the revelation making me grumpy. I know I have no claim to Libby, but I'm not ready to share her. I want her pussy all to myself, at least for a few weeks, before I have to come to terms with the fact that she's going to put her newfound sexy skills to use with another man. "Why is that so bad? What did he say?"

"He didn't say anything because as soon as I knocked on the door to his office, I choked. He asked me what was up, and I said something about the toilet paper dispenser in the kindergarten bathroom being too high for the kids, and he told me to talk it over with the janitor." Libby makes a groaning, growling sound. "The toilet paper dispenser, Justin! What the hell was I thinking? It's like my brain picked the least sexy thing it could think of just to humiliate me. I swear, sometimes it feels like my brain is not playing on my team."

"Brains are tricky like that." I plop down on the couch, trying not to sound happy about Libby's failure to secure a date with stupid Roger. "But that doesn't sound so bad, Libs. So you struck out this time. You'll do better next time."

"No, I won't," she says, breath hitching. "Because after the brilliant toilet paper dispenser comment, I stood there in the doorway staring at him, trying to get my lips to form words about Saturday night. The silence stretched on for so long that Roger finally asked me if I was feeling okay with this "why are you being so crazy, you crazy person" expression on his face. So I mumbled something about it being a long day and made a run for it, but on the way past his secretary's desk, I tripped on the carpet and fell flat on my face."

"Ouch," I say with a wince. "Are you okay?"

"No, I am not okay! I'm so embarrassed I'll never be able to step foot in the office ever again."

"Oh, come on. It's not that bad. So you fell down. People trip on things, Libby. It's part of life. I'm sure Roger has fallen down once or twice."

"It's not just the fall." Her words are muffled by the sound of a door slamming in the background, making me think she must have made it home. "It's the entire stupid interaction. Why did I have to go in there? Why did I have to get cocky and think I was ready to run before I've even learned to walk?"

"You know how to walk just fine," I say, determined to make her feel better. "Stop beating yourself up, get inside, and run yourself a bath. I'll come over in a little while, after you've had time to get nice and loose, and give you a massage. How does that sound? Just a massage, no pressure for anything else."

She sniffs. "Why? Have you changed your mind about wanting to do filthy things to me?"

"No," I scoff, "of course I haven't, I—"

"I mean, if that's what you've decided, it's fine. I get it," she says, her voice thick with emotion. "I should probably give up before I get started, right? I mean, what's the point of learning to enjoy orgasms and dirty talk and sexting and all the rest of it with a friend if I'm never going to be able to transition into being with a real person?"

"Hey! I'm real."

"I know you are, but you know what I mean." She sighs, the sound so sad and defeated that I know I have no choice but to head over to her place and ambush her with feel-good sexy times. It is my duty as an American and a gentleman and the person who has been fantasizing about this completely and utterly desirable woman for the past forty-eight hours.

If anyone can prove to her that she's got what it takes to have a fulfilling sexual and romantic relationship, it's me.

"I do *not* know what you mean." I stand, grabbing my keys from the top of the pile of mail on the kitchen island on my way toward the door. "And I'm not going to let you give up on blossoming into a full-blown sex goddess because one dink looked at you funny and made you nervous."

She sniffs again. "You really think I can blossom into a sex goddess?"

"I do. And I'm coming over right now to prove it to you." I open the door, stopping short as I see Libby standing on the other side, looking adorable and sad in a pink linen dress with a flowery scarf wrapped around her neck.

She drops her arm, letting her phone hang limply to her side. "I'm already here. I didn't feel like going home and being alone with myself and my stupid traitor brain."

"Good." I end the call and drop my phone and keys onto the table beside the door. "Get in here, sexy."

"I'm not sexy." Her lips turn down hard. "I smell like feet. After lunch, Becca gave me a hug with pimento cheese spread all over her face, but I didn't realize I'd been cheesed until the curds were dry and crusty."

"You don't smell like feet. You smell like Libby." I sniff experimentally as I take her hand and draw her inside. "And maybe a little bit like feet."

Her head falls back as her eyes close. "God, I'm sorry."

"Why are you sorry? This is an easy problem to solve." I take her backpack and her phone and set them on the table before slowly unwinding the scarf from her neck and hanging it from a nearby hook. "All we have to do is get you out of these pimento clothes."

Libby's eyes meet mine as I rest my hands on her waist, fisting the soft fabric of her dress in my hands. "Do you really think I can do this?" she asks.

"Do what?" I gather more of the dress into my fists, drawing her hemline up inch by inch "Let me undress you and make you come so many times you forget why you were sad?"

She shakes her head, holding my gaze with an

intensity that makes me even more aware of the electricity building between us. "Will I ever be able to get out of my head and stop being nervous? Will it ever feel easy or natural with anyone but you?"

A voice in my head answers "No," in a strong, steady tone, and a wave of possessiveness that has no place in a friends-with-benefits relationship rushes through my chest. But I push them both aside to assure Libby that, "Yes. It will. Just give it time." Her hemline reaches her waist, and I slip one hand beneath her dress to rest on the warm skin at the small of her back, above what feels like another pair of lace panties. Her lashes flutter as she leans into me, her breasts brushing against my chest enough to make me hard.

"But first, give *me* time," I say, my cock getting thicker as I hook my thumb over the waistband of her panties. "No more thinking about Roger or anyone else. From this moment, until the minute you step back through that door, you're mine, Collins. I want you thinking about me, and all the incredible things I'm doing to your body, and nothing else. Can you do that for me?"

"Yes." She gazes up at me with heat in her deep brown eyes, tempting me to jerk her panties down and devour her pussy right here in the foyer. "But I want to do incredible things to you, too. Will you show me? Show me what you like?"

"I will. But honestly, Libs, just standing this

close to you does incredible things to my body," I confess, my voice husky. "Now lift your arms, beautiful. I needed you naked five fucking minutes ago."

CHAPTER
Seventeen

Libby

Justin tugs my dress over my head and pulls me back into his arms, kissing me like he's been starved for the taste of my lips, scattering all the humiliations of the day in a rush of awareness.

My lips tingle and my skin prickles with electricity as my arms tighten around his neck, and he hugs me so tight my feet lift off the floor. He draws me up his body, sending fresh sizzles zipping through me as my nipples brush against the soft fabric of his flannel through my thin, lace bra.

"You taste so fucking good," he mumbles against my mouth as he carries me down the hallway into the large, open-concept kitchen and living room. "Like maple syrup and coffee and Libby. And the Libby part is the best part."

I gasp as Justin's big hand squeezes my bottom

tight, pulling me closer to where he's hard and thick, pulsing against my belly, assuring me that this isn't something he's doing out of pity. He's doing this because he wants me as much as I want him, and I'm so grateful.

The fact that a gorgeous, experienced, been-around-the-block-and-then-some man can still find me sexy and attractive is doing wonders for my confidence, but there is still so much to learn, a fact made abundantly clear as Justin lays me down on the couch, kneeling between my legs as he tugs off his sweater and undershirt and starts working open the close on his jeans.

"Here?" My eyes widen as I glance past him at the floor-to-ceiling windows and the city of Portland stretching away toward the river and the hills beyond.

"Here." He holds my gaze as he draws his zipper down, the buzz as the teeth separate enough to make my nipples pucker even tighter.

"But you don't have any blinds," I say, torn between anxiety and arousal as he steps out of his jeans, revealing a pair of tight black boxer briefs that leave nothing about his anatomy to the imagination.

"It's all right. There aren't any other buildings around here tall enough for anyone to see inside. The only one who's going to see you naked and coming on my mouth is me." He hooks his hands behind my knees, drawing me closer, until he's looming over me like a god descended from

Mount Olympus.

God, he's beautiful. And terrifying. The perfection of his body—broad shoulders, powerful chest, and an eight-pack chiseled into his abdomen—is intimidating enough, considering my own workouts consist mostly of long walks in the woods and riding my bike to the farmer's market on the weekends. But it's the seven, eight, maybe even *nine* inches straining the fabric of his boxers that make my pulse speed and my throat threaten to close up with panic.

Surely there's something wrong with him. It's not supposed to be that big.

Is it?

"Something wrong?" His hands skim gently up and down my thighs in a way that would be soothing if my heart weren't slamming against my ribs from a combination of fear and arousal.

"According to everything I've read, the average size of an erect penis in the United States is five point eight inches."

His lips curve. "Is that right? You do a lot of reading about penises, Libs?"

"I've done enough." I cast a meaningful glance south of his border. "So what's up with that?"

Amusement makes his eyes twinkle as his hands move to my waist, circling it with his fingers. "What's up with what?"

"You know what. You know exactly what. As much as you get around, you must have realized by now that that's not normal."

He laughs, the bastard, but before I can tell him to shut up and take me seriously, he says, "Don't worry. It's perfectly normal, and if we decide to go that far, there won't be any problems. I promise."

I swallow hard. "I don't like broken promises."

"I know you don't," he says, his smile fading. "I wouldn't lie to you, Libby. I promise, if you decide you want me inside you, I'm only going to make you feel good. But today, you don't have to worry about it. My abnormal cock and I have other plans for your pussy."

"I didn't mean to hurt your feelings," I say as he lengthens himself on top of me.

"You didn't." He cups my breast, teasing my nipple through my bra, making things low in my body pulse. "Being called a freak is the best thing to happen to my cock all day. He's super proud of himself."

"Well, that's nice, but there's really nothing to be proud of. It's just genetics."

"Shhhh, your logic won't work here, Collins. Cocks are notoriously immune to logic. Cocks only hear what they want to hear, and right now mine is sure that he's the biggest, sexiest bastard on the block."

I nod as my brows lift. "Do you always talk about your cock in third person?"

"Not always. Sometimes I stick a hat on him, do my best cock voice, and put on a puppet show to build morale. Maybe if you're really lucky, I'll do one for you later."

I smile against Justin's lips as he kisses me, making our teeth bump together through our skin when he smiles back. "Are you this goofy in bed with all your women?"

"I don't want to think about other women," he says, reaching beneath me to pop the clasp on my bra. "I just want to think about you, and your beautiful body, and how many times I can make you scream my name before I have to take a break to feed you dinner."

He draws my bra down my arms and tosses it on the floor, cupping my breasts in his hands and pressing them closer together, the heat in his eyes as he lowers his mouth to my tight nipples making me burn. And then his tongue sweeps across one tight, aching tip, and I catch fire.

"Oh God, Jus." I arch my back, threading my fingers into his soft hair as he sucks my nipple into his mouth. Waves of hot, sticky bliss spread through me as he torments first one breast and then the other, sucking, licking, and eventually biting my nipples until I'm squirming beneath him, desperate for him to touch me in even more intimate places. My entire pelvis is heavy, leaden with need, and my panties are so wet that I would be embarrassed if I weren't so turned on, so hungry and wild and ready for more.

I've never felt anything like this before. Not in my solo experiments with my vibrator and certainly not with Brett. When Brett touched my breasts, it had been pleasant, tingly, and interesting. Justin's erotic assault on my sensitive flesh is breathtaking, mind-blowing, nearly enough to make me come even before he slips his hand down the front of my panties. I'm so primed and ready that all it takes is the slightest brush of his calloused fingers over my clit and I explode.

I cry out, arching into his hand as my release blows through me, making me moan and heat rush from between my legs, easing Justin's way as he presses a single finger deep into my pussy. My body throbs in response, locking down tight around him as he glides in and out, his finger mimicking the rhythm of his hips as he thrusts against my thigh, letting me feel how hard and hot he still is.

"Now your turn," I say, breath still coming fast as I drift back down to earth.

"Not even close to my turn." He moves lower, kissing the curls between my legs through my panties. "It's still your turn until I say otherwise. God, I can't wait to taste you. You smell so good, Libby, so salty and wet. I love how wet you are for me, beautiful. It makes me so fucking hot."

He draws my panties down my thighs, tossing them on the floor before his hands hook behind my knees. But as he tries to spread my legs, I tense in spite of myself. The thought of Justin kissing me down there is enough to make me dizzy with wanting, but I'm also scared, anxious, and worried that maybe he's not the only abnormal one on this couch.

"Relax, Libs," Justin says softly, pressing a kiss to my knee. "It's going to feel good, I promise."

"That's not what I'm worried about," I confess.

"You don't need to be worried about anything." This time he kisses my inner thigh, making me shiver as he gently, but firmly, spreads me wide. "I want to do this for you. And for me. I want your taste in my mouth, beautiful." He kisses me higher, only inches from where my clit throbs, already desperate for more. "I can't wait to feel you lose control again, Libby. Do you know how sexy you are when you come?"

I shake my head slowly from side to side, my heart doing a slow-motion swan dive as Justin's mouth comes to hover at my apex, so close his breath warms the slick, swollen flesh between my legs.

"So, so sexy," he whispers, pausing to pull in a deeper breath. "And you smell so good."

"Are you sure? Brett only did this once and he—" I swallow hard, fighting to focus as Justin's hands come to either side of my sex, spreading my innermost lips, baring me so completely to him that a rush of adrenaline and desire makes my legs tremble. "He di-didn't like it."

"Then he was a fucking fool." His tongue sweeps out, licking slowly, deliberately up the seam of me, making me gasp as electricity shoots through me in response. "You are delicious." He holds my gaze as he circles my clit with his tongue, again and again, the intimacy of the moment so intense that I feel like my chest is going to implode.

Just as the tension spinning tight between my hipbones threatens to become something more, he pulls back, reaching up to roll my almost too-sensitive nipples with his damp fingers, summoning a pained, pleasured sound from deep in my throat.

"Here's what's going to happen," he says in a low voice as he continues to torment my breasts. "I'm going to devour your beautiful, perfect, delicious pussy, and if you want it harder or faster or slower or deeper, you're going to tell me. You're going to tell me loud and clear and make sure I hear how you want me to fuck you, Libby."

My cheeks flush hot and fast, making me even dizzier than I was before.

"Do you hear me, Libs?" Justin swirls his tongue around my clit again as my eyes slide closed and his hand glides down my ribs to my waist.

"Yes." I shudder beneath him as my body turns electric. "I heard you."

"Then tell me what you want, gorgeous. What do you want me to do?"

"Kiss me," I whisper. "There."

"How, baby? How do you want me to kiss you?"

"Hard. And deep," I say, pulse spiking as the uncharacteristically demanding words escape my lips. "I want to feel your tongue inside of me."

"I want that, too. So fucking much." Justin digs his fingers into my hips. "Keep it up, baby. Keep telling me what you want because all I want is to make you feel good. To make you come harder than you've ever come before."

My lips part to confess that he already has, but before I can speak his mouth covers my sex and his tongue swirls around my entrance, kissing my pussy every bit as intimately as he kissed my mouth, and my vocabulary is reduced to a long, low moan.

And then a gasp and then his name, which I chant again and again as he takes me higher, higher, until I shatter into a thousand perfectly broken pieces.

CHAPTER
Eighteen

Justin

The moment she arches beneath me, her body stiffening as she starts to come, I angle my head and drive my tongue deeper into her pussy, swirling against her inner walls as wet heat fills my mouth. She tastes like the ocean, where lava meets the sea, hot, tart, alive, and sexy as ever-loving fuck.

"Yes, Libby," I murmur, suckling her clit, drawing out her release until she's twisting and writhing beneath me. But I wrap my arms around her thighs and hold her prisoner to her own pleasure, keeping her pinned until she reaches down to claw at my shoulders with a ragged sob.

"Now you. Please, Justin, I need to make you come. I need to make you feel the way I feel right now."

I sit back on my heels, intending to get out of

my boxer briefs as fast as humanly possible, but before I can reach for my waistband, Libby's fingers curl around the fabric, pulling it down, freeing my cock. My breath catches as she takes me in hand, wrapping her fingers around my suffering length, making it twitch.

I can't remember the last time I was this desperate for a woman's touch. Libby's cool fingers as she explores my swollen flesh, squeezing and stroking until I groan, are messengers of pleasure and mercy. And then she lowers her head, and my groan becomes a curse and a silent prayer for the strength to keep from losing control until I've had the chance to properly enjoy her mouth on my cock.

Her tongue circles my sensitive tip, licking away the pre-come that's been leaking steadily out of me since the first time I made her come. "Here's what's going to happen," she says, her breath warm on my shaft. "I'm going to devour your gorgeous, delicious cock, and you're going to tell me how you like it."

I smile as I recognize my own words from a few minutes ago, feeling oddly proud of her. But I guess it isn't odd for a teacher to feel pride when a student catches on exceptionally quickly.

"You're going to tell me if you want it harder or faster," she continues, circling my head again, and again, until my balls start to feel like leaden weights dragging between my legs. "Or slower or deeper."

"Right now I just want to be inside your mouth, beautiful." I thread my right hand into her silky hair. "I'm dying for it, in fact. So any way you want to do that is incredible by me."

"All right." Her lips part and a moment later she begins to slide her mouth down, sucking me deeper, making my vision blur because it is so crazy hot to watch my cock pushing past Libby's pink lips. She pauses about halfway down, her tongue working against my skin as she glides down another half inch, but I stop her before she can take me deeper, fisting my fingers lightly in her hair.

"That's good," I say, my voice thick and my dick pulsing hard between her lips. "Don't push if it's uncomfortable. That feels amazing just like that, and if you want you can use your hand for the rest."

She brings her hand to the base of my cock and squeezes. As she pulls back, her fist follows behind her mouth, drawing out the sweet pressure on my length. "Yes, Libs, just like that. That's so insanely good."

She repeats the same sinful up and down, three, four, five times until I can't help but pulse my hips forward as her mouth closes around me. She sucks me deeper in response, increasing the suction, making me so wild I know I'm not going to be able to stay in control much longer.

"Just your hand now, Libs. Just use your hand."

"But I want more of you," she says in this rough, sexy voice that goes straight to my suffering balls. "I want to feel you come in my mouth."

Fuck, and that's it. All I can handle.

I haul her up my body by her hair, fusing my mouth to hers as I guide her hand back to my cock and cover it with mine. "That's sexy as hell," I growl against her lips as I show her the rhythm that feels right. "But not this time. I don't want to hurt you."

"You weren't hurting me." She takes over, tugging on my cock as I cup her breast, squeezing it in my hand as she jerks me with the perfect speed, the perfect pressure.

"But I could have. Let's save deep throating for lesson eight or nine. It's advanced subject matter." I groan as she tightens her grip. "God, yes, like that. Oh fuck, Libby, that's perfect. You're making me crazy."

I thrust in her hand as she kisses me hard and deep, her breath coming faster as I catch her nipple between my thumb and palm and squeeze. "I can't wait to feel you go," she says, moaning as I transfer my attention to her other breast. "I want yours as much as I wanted mine. I can't wait to feel you lose control."

"Yes, baby," I groan, slamming into her hand, so close my thighs are starting to shake. "Keep talking to me, Libby. Keep talking while you jerk my cock. Tell me what you want me to do to you, all the ways you want me to touch you."

"I want you to suck my nipples," she says, breath rushing over my lips. "I want your teeth on my breasts and my neck."

"Yes, God, yes." My eyes squeeze shut, pressure building to the breaking point.

"I love feeling your teeth on my skin." Libby's hand moves faster, and my fingers squeeze her breast tight. "And then I want your fingers inside me. Nothing has ever felt as good as your fingers and your tongue inside me, Justin. I can't wait to feel your mouth on me again, I can't—"

Her words are drowned out by the strangled, blissed-out, choking, moaning coming sounds I make as I explode in her hand, come shooting out of me with such force that some of it ends up on Libby's chest. I glance down, my orgasm still rocking through me as I watch my release roll down her right tit onto the soft curve of her belly, deciding right then that I've never seen anything sexier than Libby naked with my come on her breasts.

My orgasm lays waste to me, leaving me so spent that I barely have the energy to pull Libby on top of me before I collapse back onto the couch.

"I'm messy." She tenses as our chests touch, transferring some of my stickiness from her skin to mine.

"I love it," I breathe, kissing her until she relaxes against me. "I want to lie here sticky and sweaty with you for a few minutes, if that's all right."

"It's completely all right." She props up on one arm, gazing down at me with a smile curving her lips. "So I guess that was all right, too?"

"So much better than all right." I sigh as I hug her closer.

She taps a nail on my bare shoulder. "You promise? It was really good? You're not blowing smoke up my butt?"

"No, I'm squeezing your butt." I drop a hand to her bottom, gripping her right cheek tight. "You have a phenomenal ass, by the way. Almost as nice as your breasts."

"Thank you." She nibbles her bottom lip before adding in a softer voice. "That was only my second time doing that. But I watched some videos last night, so I was hoping it would be okay."

"Firstly—again, it was far, far better than okay. Secondly—what kind of videos?" I wiggle my brows suggestively. "You mean porn?"

Her blush spreads from her cheeks down the pale column of her throat. "Instructional videos."

"By which you mean porn."

She rolls her eyes with a huff. "Fine. Yes. Porn, but it was good porn. There was a story line."

"Because that's why we all watch porn. For the story line." I grin, patting her bottom. "I've always enjoyed teasing you, but it's even more fun when I can watch you blush all the way down to your chest."

"Stop it," she says, shaking her head. "You're the worst. And just so you know, even the porn actor I saw barely had more than seven inches."

"I think your nipples are blushing."

"Shut it, Cruise!" Her nose wrinkles until her face is screwed into a cranky expression that is almost unbearably cute.

"I would check the heat level of your nipples with my mouth if your breasts weren't covered in come."

She pokes me in the shoulder, harder this time. "And whose fault is that?"

"Mine, all mine," I say, grinning. "And yours, for sucking and jerking me off like a fucking porn star."

She lifts her chin, staring down her nose at me. "Fine. If you're going to tease me, then the next time I won't do my homework, and I'll probably end up tripping my gag reflex or something sexy like that."

"No, you'll do your homework," I say in a stern voice. "As an educator, I refuse to tolerate shoddy study habits in this classroom."

"Is that right?" Her lips press together as she fights a smile. "And what are you going to do if I start falling behind in class, professor?"

"I suppose I'll have to punish you, Miss Collins." I hold her gaze as I run my palm over the curve of her ass to her thigh and then back up to her waist, loving the spark that lights her eyes when she realizes what I'm playing at. "I might have to lift up your skirt, pull down your panties, and show you what happens to students with poor study habits. What do you think about that?"

She looks up and to the left, pretending to seriously consider my question. "Um, I think that could be…interesting."

I arch a brow. "Interesting, huh?"

She shrugs. "I think so. Maybe for lesson five or six."

"So, in your twisted little mind, spanking and role play come several lessons before deep throating?"

Uncertainty flickers across her features. "Maybe? Is that weird?"

"Nothing is weird as long as it's what you really want," I say, the teasing note vanishing from my tone. "But make sure it's something that really turns you on, not just something you think turns me on. I know some men feel differently, but I don't want you to do anything with me that you're not totally into. Making you hot is the thing that makes me crazy."

Her gaze softens. "You're a very generous person. And lover."

"You're blushing again," I say, laughing as she slaps my shoulder.

"I'm starting to think spanking *you* should be lesson two."

"Then let's hit the shower, baby, and you can redden my ass with the flat side of my back scrubber. It'll make a great paddle."

She laughs, pretending to still be angry with me as I carry her into the shower. But by the time the spray is warm, we're kissing again and then there is more coming in the shower and in my bed and back on the couch, where we get sidetracked on the way to raiding the fridge for Leftovers Dinner.

I'm having so much fun that I really don't want Libby to go, but I finally walk her down to the parking garage around ten, after extracting promises of a sleepover very soon.

"Tomorrow night," she promises. "You can come over as soon as I get back from my knitting circle."

"I'll come with you to your knitting circle," I say, not wanting to be apart from Libby or her pussy any more than absolutely necessary. "I've got practice early, but I'll be free by four."

She nods slowly, her eyes narrowing. "Okay. But you'll be the only man. I assume that's okay with you?"

"Totally okay. I like women. You in particular." And then I kiss her some more, until I've got her pinned between me and her car door and I'm seriously considering making her come again in the parking garage. But the elevator opens before I can slip my hand down the front of her pants, and Libby pulls away with a wicked grin.

"Tomorrow," she says. "I'll pick you up at four thirty. Remember to bring your work in progress. And your toothbrush."

"See you then." I kiss her one last time, lingering on her sweet lips, and then I let her go, feeling like a lucky bastard. In less than twenty-four hours she'll be all mine again, and tomorrow night I won't have to say good-bye.

CHAPTER
Nineteen

Libby

Joining a knitting and crochet circle can be an empowering and heartwarming experience.

I've been a part of politically active circles that brainstormed ways to aid the re-election efforts of our favorite education commissioner, and charity-minded circles that knitted caps for babies in the NICU. I helped coordinate a knit-in—a group of forty women who took turns knitting around the clock for a week outside the Oregon Arts Council office to raise awareness of the oft-neglected needlecraft arts—and secured funding for after-school knitting groups across the greater Portland area. And just two summers ago, I joined a group of handicraft-minded craft brew enthusiasts. We meet four times a year to sample the latest micro-brews selected by our fearless leader, Mindy, and spend a long afternoon seeing who can hook the most adorable beer-themed project.

Bottom line: I'm no babe in the woods when it comes to socializing with yarn.

But in recent weeks, my current knitting group has gone off the rails a bit. The introduction of two coordination-impaired newbies and a woman who insists on large-format knitting—using PVC pipe to knit massive installation pieces for her gallery—has put a strain on the usually cozy and boisterous dynamic. Tempers have flared, snark has flown, and Edna, our seventy-year-old host, threatened to put the box wine away last week if Priscilla, the self-absorbed PVC princess, didn't stop jabbing people with her pipes every time she got to the end of a row.

I have no idea how the girls are going to react to me showing up with six feet three inches of hot hooking hockey player on my arm, but I'm imagining it's not going to be a calm and collected affair.

"Just be super sweet to Edna," I whisper as Justin and I make our way up the cobbled walkway in front of Edna's adorable craftsman bungalow. "And don't ask too many questions. The newbies are already driving her crazy. Hannah had to be shown how to cast on four different times last week."

"Who do you think you're talking to, Libs?" Justin rolls a crochet hook from his messenger bag around one finger like a gunslinger spinning a revolver. "This isn't my first time at the crochet rodeo. I'm a fucking professional. A seasoned pro."

I snort. "Is this the same seasoned pro who nearly had a breakdown working a garden trellis afghan pattern last year and called me at midnight on Christmas Eve to come over and untangle his mess?"

"That pattern was hairy as balls, Collins." Justin points his hook accusingly my way. "And it was for my mother's Christmas present. I wanted it to be fucking perfect, okay?"

"You kiss your mother with that mouth?" I ask, lifting a wry brow.

"Not lately, but I may have kissed you once or twice."

Before I realize he's making a move, Justin pulls me off the path into the shadows of a giant camellia bush and crushes his lips to mine. And even though I know I should tell him to stop—I don't want anyone in my circle to get the wrong idea about the nature of our relationship—I can't help but kiss him back. It's like the moment his tongue sweeps into my mouth, I lose all capacity for rational thought and turn into a simmering, bubbling, steaming caldron of happy sex hormones.

I wrap my arms around his neck and press tight against his hard chest and think salacious thoughts about how delicious he looks naked and wonder why on earth I didn't call in sick to knitting circle and keep him clothes-less in my bed all night.

Because you're not ready for real sex, right? Or so you keep telling yourself.

I would argue that your perpetually damp panties tell a different story, Collins…

"God, I want to eat you alive," Justin growls against my lips between kisses. "You taste so good."

"I've been thinking about last night all day," I confess, fresh arousal surging through me as Justin's fingers dig into my bottom through my pants, pulling my hips closer to where he's thicker than he was a moment ago. "And how incredible you taste. I want to kiss you there again tonight, but this time I want you to finish in my mouth."

"Are you trying to kill me?" He nips my bottom lip as I pulse my hips closer to his erection, amazed that he can get me this keyed up so quickly. "You are, aren't you?"

I laugh, a husky sound that becomes a soft gasp as Justin captures my nipple through my dress. "Stop it." I cover his hand with mine but lack the will power to push it away. "No nipple touching in public."

"Oh, but you can talk about sucking my cock and grind on me through our clothes until I'm so crazy I'm ready to take you under this bush?" He kisses me again, drawing me closer to the camellia. "Come on, Libs. Let's sixty-nine under this bush for a while before we go inside."

I giggle again. "Gross. No."

"Worried about mud on your clothes?"

"I'm worried about being arrested for public indecency." I bring my hands to his chest and fist my fingers in his soft blue sweater. "Come on, let's get inside. We're already running late."

"I need five more minutes of dirty talk in the dark."

"The sooner we get inside, the sooner we can make our excuses for leaving early and head back to my place," I say, walking my fingers up to his neck to weave into his soft hair. "And the offer to stay the night still stands, as long as we get to sleep by ten and you let me out of bed at five forty-five to get dressed for work."

"Done." He releases me with a final squeeze of my bottom. "I have to be at practice at seven anyway. It's allegedly optional, but after my crap ass performance at practice last week, I know coach expects me to be there."

"But you had an amazing game." I straighten my clothes, doing my best to look like I haven't been making out in Edna's bushes.

"One amazing game. I'm not out of the woods yet." He takes my hand, threading his fingers through mine as we start up the path. "Though, I think those dirty texts were my good luck charm on Tuesday. You should sext me during the game on Saturday, and we can test my hypothesis."

I smile. "I think that could be arranged, but we probably shouldn't walk in holding hands. We don't want to give people the wrong idea."

"Oh, right." He drops my hand with seeming reluctance. "Sorry. I didn't realize we were keeping this a secret from your knitting friends, too."

"It seems best to keep it a secret from everyone, don't you think? I mean, if we were both normal people, it might not be a big deal, but you're famous. People like to talk about your love life, and when people talk about your love life, Laura is one of the first people who gets the memo."

He grunts. "True. She texted me about you today, by the way. Wanted me to call you and convince you to come to the game on Saturday. I didn't realize you were on the fence about it."

I stomp up the steps to the front porch with a little more force than necessary, wishing Laura had picked another time to get militant about herding me back into the dating pool. "I wouldn't be on the fence if she would just let me come watch you guys play. She's determined to put me in a room filled with single men on top of it. And you know her. I'm sure the plan goes deeper than simply putting me in close proximity to several eligible penises. She's got something else up her sleeve—like setting me up on a blind date without my knowledge, the way she did last summer with the guy who delivers beer to the restaurant below her apartment—and I'd really rather skip the embarrassment and stress."

"Then I'll get you a ticket down near the ice." As I ring the doorbell, he rests his hand at the small of my back before he seems to remember we're on a no-touching basis for a few hours and pulls it away. "I want you to come. I mean, assuming you want to."

"Of course I do." I glance up at him, wondering at the odd note in his voice, but before I can ask if something's bothering him, the door opens and Edna loudly announces—

"Well, now, look at this! Who is this tall drink of water, Elizabeth? And where have you been hiding him?"

"You must be Edna." Justin leans down, moving into Edna's open arms for a hug. "I'm Justin, Libby's friend. She taught me how to crochet when I was in high school."

"Oh, thank goodness." Edna pats him on the arm as he pulls away. "I don't think I could handle another newbie, especially one with big clumsy hands. No offense."

"None taken, and my hands aren't clumsy, I promise. Are they Libby?"

Thoughts of all the inspired, deft, erotic things his hands did to me last night shimmy through my thoughts and my cheeks flush. "No, they aren't. They're quite clever hands." Clever and kind and so skilled at making my body come to life that I'm starting to feel like a completely new person. A sexier, more self-assured person who managed to wave at Roger in the cafeteria today and wish him a happy Wednesday without any weirdness or self-conscious mumbling.

For more people, that would be a sad milestone, indeed, but in my world it's definitely progress.

"Excellent." Edna traps Justin's palm between both of hers and nods seriously. "In that case, we might invite you back next time, assuming you're house trained."

Justin laughs and assures her that he is, and Edna leads us into her spacious, wood-paneled living room, where an odd but comfortable assortment of chairs are arranged in a big circle around the refreshment table. The Frank Sinatra Pandora channel is working its warm, croony magic in the background, and the air smells of wool, firewood crackling in the fireplace, and freshly baked chocolate chip cookies.

It would be a purely welcoming scene if it weren't for the blond girl near the piano who looks like she's about to cry—a newbie, I can't remember her name, but her stress levels make me look positively laid-back in comparison—Dana the drag queen scowling at Priscilla with murder in her dark brown eyes, and Priscilla wonking away with her giant pipes by the fire, taking up so much room that three of our older members are practically sitting on top of each other on a green loveseat, hemmed in against the far wall.

I have only a moment to observe the obvious

distress of the assembly at large before the group notices Justin and fluttering, swooning, obnoxiously feminine sounds fill the air.

The next twenty minutes pass in a confused blur as practically everyone in the room offers to pull up a chair next to theirs for Justin—or sit on the floor by his feet in the case of Edna's teenage granddaughter, Britta, who at sixteen is easily ten times more confident around hot as heck menfolk as I've been at any age. We finally get Jus situated in a recliner not far from Priscilla, but hopefully out of jabbing range, and I snag a seat on another love seat next to the newbie, patting her on the knee encouragingly as I settle in and praise the purple-turd-looking thing emerging from her needles, which I'm assuming is going to be a scarf someday.

"I can't believe you're really here," Britta chirps to Justin, pulling her phone out of her knitting bag. "I follow you on Instagram! I love your feed so, so much."

"Oh. Well, thanks." Justin casts a slightly flustered look my way. I answer him with an "I told you so" smirk. I warned him way back when that there could be uncomfortable consequences to posing nearly naked on social media. Seeing him squirm in his chair as an under-aged girl pulls up his latest shot on her phone—Jus standing on his porch in a scarf and jeans and nothing else—and passes it around the circle is poetic justice at its finest.

"I knitted three beanies last year for your hats for the homeless drive," Britta prattles on, "and I'm already figuring out what to work on for this year. It was amazing to see how many hats you got."

"Yeah, it was amazing. Thanks for being a part of it." Jus smiles at the clearly besotted teen before fetching his current project from his messenger bag. "So, what's everyone working on? I'm halfway through a unicorn hat for my friend's daughter, and then I'm going to start on some Star Wars stuff."

We go around the circle, introducing ourselves and our works in progress, and I learn that Melanie, the newbie next to me, is indeed struggling with a scarf. I offer to help her adjust her tension—she's got her yarn so tight she can barely get the tip of the needle through to loop another stich—so I'm distracted when Priscilla starts her description of her latest piece. But by the time she rises from her chair to sashay over to Justin to offer him a closer look at the net she's working on for her Catchers of Men series, I'm picking up on the pick-up attempt loud and clear.

"The installation is going to feature mannequins tangled in the nets I've knitted," Priscilla says, holding up her work, until it becomes a screen separating her and Justin from the rest of the group. "They'll hang from the ceiling to give the viewer the sensation that he might be snatched up in a net any moment. It's going to be a really visceral, almost claustrophobic experience. I'd love to have you over to take a look at things before opening night. It's so rare to meet a man who's into sports *and* needlework. I'd love to get your unique take on the piece."

On the word "unique" she presses her hand to Justin's chest, above his pectoral muscle, but a little lower than his shoulder.

It's a weird place to touch someone, I think critically, even as I try not to let the fact that Priscilla is fondling Justin like a piece of meat get to me. Justin and I are here as friends, and he's free to allow himself to be fondled by anyone he pleases. And as irritating as she is, Pris is very, *very* pretty. With her long, blond hair, willowy figure, and cosmopolitan style, she's actually way more Justin's type than I am. It makes sense that the two most beautiful people in the room should gravitate toward each other.

I'm trying to get used to the idea that Justin might decide Priscilla is worth taking out for a test date when he leans down to dig through his bag, casually brushing her hand away from his chest in the process.

"Sounds interesting, but I'm crazy busy this time of year," he says, pulling out another ball of yarn he clearly doesn't need at this point in his work. "But you should ask Libby to go. She's got an amazing eye for art. The kids in her class place in the elementary art show every year, even though they're the youngest in their division. Don't they, Libs?"

"They do," I say, not missing the glare Pris shoots my way. "But you can't really compare kindergarten level projects with what Priscilla does at her gallery. I'm sure I wouldn't have much of value to contribute, but if you want me to swing by next week, Pris, I can."

"Don't worry about it." Priscilla's lips curve in a constipated looking grin as she sways back to her seat. "But that's so kind of you to offer. You are such a sweetheart, Libby. The little people you teach are so lucky to have you there to wipe their noses and kiss their booboos."

"Thanks," I say, her comment leaving a sour taste in my mouth.

On the surface it seems like a nice thing to say, but I can't help feeling like she intended the comment to make me feel small. Dana has been trying to instruct me on the finer points of shade—even though she insists that most white people struggle with the concept of shade, as well as its proper execution—but my shade-dar still isn't the best. I make a mental note to ask Dana later if I was shaded, and to inquire as to how I might have shaded Priscilla in return if I were of the mind to retaliate in kind, and turn my attention back to my afghan.

The conversation turns to the holidays, and all the things Edna and the other older ladies are knitting for their grandchildren. Justin breaks the rule about asking for help—wondering aloud if there's a faster way to attach the rainbow mane to his hat—but Edna's so charmed by the fact that this big, manly man is making a rainbow unicorn hat for a little girl he loves that she invites him over to the couch for up close and personal guidance. Britta swings by the love seat to ask more questions about Justin and how long I've known him, and Melanie and I end up finding common ground in the fact that we were both homeschooled as kids due to speech delays and stuttering issues.

"I had no idea." Britta frowns up at me from her place on the floor. "You always seem so chill and collected."

"Do I?" I ask, surprised.

"Totally. You're super classy," Britta says, popping her gum. "Like Audrey Hepburn or one of those old movie stars. My friend Kelly is, too. I can't pull that off, though. I talk too much, and I cuss pretty much constantly." Her blue eyes widen as she casts a quick glance over her shoulder to where Edna is now helping Hannah, the other newbie, pick up a dropped stitch, and she turns back to add in a softer voice, "But don't tell Gran. She would wash my mouth out with soap. I mean, everybody does it at my school, but she's super old-fashioned about stuff like that."

"We won't tell," Melanie assures her with a smile, looking much more comfortable than she did when Jus and I walked in. "And I agree, I never would have thought you used to have a stutter, Libby. You're always so gracious and put together."

"Well, thank you." I laugh self-consciously. "That's sweet of you to say."

Their words make me wonder if I maybe I'm not as much of a hopeless case as I think I am. Maybe my nervous moments don't show as much on the outside as I've assumed. And maybe, once I've learned all the things Justin wants to teach me, I will truly be ready to start dating like a normal twenty-something.

It should be an encouraging thought, but as I head into the kitchen to make a fresh batch of lemonade for Edna, I'm not encouraged. Or excited. Or looking forward to spreading my wings and jumping out of the friends-with-benefits nest. I want to stay in the nest, with Justin, and shut out the rest of the world.

I'm wondering if that's bad news—a sign that maybe I'm getting too attached to something Justin and I both agreed should remain casual— when a high voice behind me sing-songs, "Hey there, Libby, darling. Can we talk?" making me flinch so hard I slosh water over the rim of the pitcher and into the sink.

"Sorry to scare you," Priscilla says as I shut off the faucet.

"No, it's my fault. I was lost in thought." I laugh as I set the pitcher down and reach for the lemonade packet from the cupboard. "What did you want to talk about? If you changed your mind and want me to come by the gallery, I really don't mind at all. I know I'm not a professional, but I've been going to museums and openings since I was a kid. My parents are big supporters of art of all kinds."

"Maybe I will ask you to swing by." Pris crosses her arms as she leans her hip against the solid oak dining table on the left side of the kitchen. "But I was actually coming to ask you about Justin. Is he seeing anyone, that you know of?"

"Um…" I blink what I hope is innocently as I open the lemonade packet and pour it into the pitcher, figuring it's best to keep my eyes elsewhere as I lie to Pris. "Not that I know of. But he just broke up with a woman he was dating for a while, so I'm not sure he's looking to get involved with anyone right now."

Priscilla chuckles. "Oh, I'm not looking to get involved, either. Just looking for someone who can keep up with me in the bedroom, and Justin looks like he might have potential, you know?"

"Oh, well…" I stir the lemonade with an intensity and focus that would be more appropriate for performing open-heart surgery. I don't know Pris well enough to be comfortable having this kind of conversation, and I sure as heck don't want to discuss Justin's bedroom "potential" with her or anyone else.

I'm still trying to figure out what to say to kill

this line of questioning without being rude, when she laughs.

"Don't worry about it, Libby. I shouldn't have asked. I had a feeling that kind of question would make you uncomfortable." She makes a concerned, cooing sound so falsely sweet it makes my tongue curl. "You don't date much, do you? I mean, you never talk about a significant other. It's all kids and crafts with you, huh?"

"Kids and crafts are a big part of my life," I admit, rinsing the wooden spoon I used to mix the lemonade and preparing to flee the kitchen posthaste.

I also have a sister I go to art shows and concerts with, friends, family, and volunteer work, and a deep love for long hikes in the woods, but Priscilla doesn't really want to know about my life. She wants to build herself up by making someone else feel small and strange, but I refuse to give her the satisfaction.

"And that's great," she says, still in that patronizing voice that makes me want to splash lemonade in her eye. "Not everyone is a sexual being. Our culture would have you believe differently, but I know plenty of women like you. Some men, too. There are lots of people who are perfectly content to live quiet, sexless lives."

"It's been nice chatting with you," I lie again, going for a personal record for number of falsehoods in a row. "But I should probably get back to the circle before people get thirsty."

"Are you okay?" Pris angles in front of me, blocking my path.

"I'm fine," I chirp, throat tight.

"I didn't mean to upset you. Seriously, Libby, there's nothing to be embarrassed about."

"I'm not embarrassed." I look at the antique globe light fixture on the ceiling and then the collection of framed rooster prints and paintings on the wall, anywhere but at Priscilla's stupid, falsely sympathetic face.

"Unless you wish things were different." She steps closer, lowering her voice. "Unless you were hoping that one day Justin was going to realize that you've had a crush on him for years and decide he wants to be more than friends."

I cut my burst of laughter short by clearing my throat. "I need to go."

"It's okay, Libby. We've all had crushes on people who don't—"

"I haven't had a crush on Justin for years, Priscilla." I'm about to tell her that even if I had, I wouldn't be talking about my feelings for Justin or anyone else with her, when she cuts in with a sly smile.

"So it's a recent development, then?"

"No!" I huff.

"Right." She smirks. "Your cheeks just turned bright red."

"So? I'm uncomfortable talking about a friend behind his back." I curse my stupid face for making it look like I'm lying.

I'm not lying! I don't have a crush on Justin. I just want to be naked in bed with him all the time, find his jokes funnier than they used to be, and my chest got all warm watching him make a gift for a little girl he cares about. And maybe earlier tonight I had another passing thought about what kind of father he might be, and decided again that he would probably be pretty wonderful. But that doesn't mean I want to be more than friends…

Does it?

Oh my God…

Does it? Am I starting to want more than friends-with-benefits? And if so, what the heck am I going to do about it? I don't want to call things off now. I need more time, more Justin, more long nights with nothing but his mouth and his hands and the way his body fits so perfectly against mine.

"Okay, okay." Pris lifts her hands innocently at her sides, as if she hasn't just thrown a major wrench in my nice, uncomplicated sex education. "But if you decide you need to talk, you have my number. I'm a good listener."

"Thank you." I stare down at the pitcher of lemonade in my hands, feeling terrible. Maybe I misjudged Priscilla, and she really is trying to help. Maybe the patronizing tone and the certainty that I'm being judged and found pathetic are all in my head.

"Of course. We've all been there, you know."

"Been where?" I murmur, gaze fixed on the tiny bubbles on the surface of the lemonade.

"Hung up on someone who's totally out of our league."

Before I can pour the entire pitcher of lemonade over Priscilla's mean, self-esteem destroying head, Justin's voice sounds from the doorway behind her.

"Hey, there you are," he says, breezing around Pris like she's not even there. "I've been looking for you everywhere, beautiful."

And then he takes the pitcher from my hands and sets it on the table, pulls me into his arms, and proceeds to kiss me like my mouth is the most delicious thing he's encountered in his twenty-eight years on earth. The kiss is slow and deep, with his tongue stroking against mine as his hands smooth down to cup my bottom through my dress.

For a moment, I'm too shocked to respond, but then I realize he must have heard my conversation with Priscilla, and I melt gratefully into him, twining my arms around his neck and hugging him even closer.

Oh, this man is a good man. A good, sweet, kind man who would do anything for a friend, including kiss her senseless in front of a big, mean jerk.

By the time we finally come up for air, I'm dizzy, and my body is humming with the need to get out of here, get Justin alone, and show him how thankful I am for the wonder that he is.

"I'm ready to go, how about you?" he asks.

"Very ready," I glance over his shoulder at the now empty kitchen. "I guess Priscilla decided to give us a few minutes alone."

"Good. I didn't want to call her a fucking bitch to her face, but I might not have been able to restrain myself." His muscles flex as he pulls my hips closer to his, making my breath catch as I feel the evidence of his need pulsing against my stomach. "If anyone's out of their league here, it's me, Libs."

"Not true, but thank you." I press a hand to his scruffy cheek as a wave of emotion swells in my chest, different from anything I've felt for Jus before. "For that, and for coming to my rescue."

"Always," he promises, with a sincerity that makes the emotion swell a little bigger. "Let's get out of here. I need to be naked with you."

I nod, not trusting my voice. I need to be naked with him, too, and not because I want to learn more about sex, or because I want to build up my confidence for the man who will come into my life when Justin and I are through. I need it because I need to show Justin how much he means to me, how much I treasure him and love giving him pleasure. I need it because my life is a darker place without him in it and because I have never felt more at home than I do when I'm in his arms.

Pretty sure that's the definition of making love, Libs,

not hot, no-strings-attached sex, my inner voice helpfully points out.

The voice is right, but I can't bring myself to worry about the implications of that right now. As I take Justin's hand, holding tight as we collect our things and say our good-byes, all I can think about is how lucky I am to get to be with him, even if it's only for a little while.

CHAPTER
Twenty

Justin

We don't talk in the car, and when we get back to Libby's place we don't bother turning on the lights. We slam the door, drop our shit on the floor, and come together—swift and urgent—in the dark. Her lips crash into mine and her warm curves mold against my chest as I draw her up and guide her legs around my waist, my entire body catching fire.

"Bedroom," she murmurs against my lips as her arms lock around my neck, making it clear she's not letting go until we both get what we need. "Now."

"Yes, ma'am." I squeeze her ass tight with one hand as I drive the other into her hair, fisting the silky strands as I kiss her hard and deep. She's so petite I have no trouble holding her with one arm, a fact that reminds me how tight she was on my finger last night, even after she had already come on my tongue.

I'm going to have to go slow, or I'm going to hurt her, and the last thing I want to do is hurt Libby. All I want to do is make her feel good, to show her that she is sexy and beautiful and, even more importantly, fun and silly and thoughtful and classy and a hundred other things that make her the kind of woman any man would be lucky to call his.

Including this man…

As I move swiftly through Libby's darkened apartment, devouring her mouth as I carry her to the bedroom, I realize there's no use trying to deny it anymore. I don't want to be friends with benefits or to keep this a secret or to help Libby grow confident enough to start a relationship with someone else. I want her to be mine. I want her to think of me the way she thinks of Roger, as someone who might be good enough to go all the way with a woman like her.

And I don't just mean sex. I mean her time and attention and maybe someday her heart.

That's not our agreement, not anywhere close, but I can't help myself. I don't plan on fucking Libby tonight. I'm going to make love to her, to show her with every touch, every kiss, every stroke of my body inside hers that I can be good for her and that this thing growing between us is worth giving a real shot.

"No lessons tonight." I lay her down on the

bed and cover her with my body, loving the way she keeps her arms and legs wrapped around me, pulling me closer. "I just want to be with you. Just you and me and whatever feels right."

"Sounds perfect." She slips her hands beneath my shirt, her fingers cool on my stomach. "Can we get naked now? I think naked will feel very right."

"Agreed." My lips curve as I pull back, stripping off my sweater and undershirt and then moving to help Libby tug her dress and the tight white shirt beneath over her head. Our socks, shoes, and pants do a similar vanishing act and then I'm back in Libby's arms, with nothing separating us except my boxer briefs and her panties.

Well, and her bra, but that isn't long for this world.

I reach behind her, popping the clasp between her shoulder blades and easing the straps down her arms, slowly baring her full breasts. They are alabaster in the streetlight filtering through the curtains and so perfect they look like they could have been carved from marble. But she's not made of stone, my Libby. She is soft and warm and when I draw her nipple into my mouth and swirl my tongue around her tightened tip, she tastes like paradise.

She's the ocean on a day without any responsibilities. She's fresh air and hope and happiness that is carnal and innocent at the same time. I want to do filthy things to this woman, but somehow I know no matter how down and dirty we get, on some level being with her will always be sweet.

Because she's Libby, and I love her.

I do, I love her. And maybe not just as a friend. Not anymore.

"I want you so much." She arches into my mouth as I transfer my attention to her left nipple, licking and sucking as I roll the other tight, damp tip between my fingers. "I want all of you. Inside me. Please."

"I want that, too," I say, wincing as my need spikes so hard and fast it's almost painful. "But I need you wet, Libs."

"I'm already wet." She takes my hand, guiding it between her legs, making me groan as I feel how hot and slick she is. "All I could think about on the ride home was how much I need to be with you like this. I need you inside me so badly it feels like I'm going to die if it doesn't happen, Jus."

"It's going to happen," I assure her, the thought of pushing my pulsing cock inside her enough to make my head spin. "But you're going to come for me first, baby. I need you even wetter. I don't want to hurt you, not even a little bit."

"It's okay. I know it might—" Her breath rushes out as I begin to circle her clit with my thumb. "I know, I… I…"

"Yes?" I draw her legs farther apart as I kiss my way down her belly, replacing my thumb with my mouth and swirling my tongue around the small, tight nub at the top of her stunning pussy.

"There's something I should tell you." Her fingers fist in the quilt beneath her as she presses closer to my mouth. "God, how do you do that?"

"Do what?" I suckle her clit lightly, loving the way she cries out in response.

"Make me crazy so fast?" Her breasts rise and fall as her breath begins to come in swift, shallow gasps. "It's so good, Jus. So amazing I almost can't believe it's real."

My next swirl ends with a deep plunge of my tongue into her pussy. And fuck, she's as delicious as she was last night, so delicious I can't stop myself from driving into her pussy again and again, deeper and deeper, until I'm fucking her with my tongue while I rub her clit with my fingers and she writhes against me, demanding her pleasure in a way that makes me even hotter.

Fuck, yes. This is how I want Libby to feel— free, wild, shameless, and determined to take what she needs from me. I live to serve her pleasure, to get her off, to know I'm the one making her lose control.

She calls my name, pressing closer to my mouth, and I reach up, palming her breasts, trapping her nipples tight between my fingers.

A beat later, she detonates.

I can feel the moment she goes—the way her

muscles pull tight and her hips lift powerfully into my mouth—and then her wetness flows over my tongue, making me groan. She tastes so good, so primal and sexy, that I want to lap up every drop, but instead I force my mouth from between her legs, tugging off my boxers as I reach for my discarded jeans at the foot of the bed. I jerk out my wallet, rip open the condom wrapper inside, and guide the rubber over my cock, gritting my teeth as it rolls over my hypersensitive tip.

I'm so turned on, so desperate to be with Libby, that it feels like every nerve ending in my body has been buffed with sandpaper. I'm raw and aching and the only cure is to get inside her, to push into her heat and let her bring me in out of the cold.

I move over her, kissing her with the taste of her body still salty and sweet on my tongue. She wraps her arms around me and spreads her legs, pressing her wetness to the thick ridge of my cock, silently asking for what we both need.

"Yes, beautiful," I mumble against her lips as I fit my erection to her entrance. "I can't wait to be inside you, Libby. I need you so much."

"Me, too," she whispers. "So much."

I glide slowly forward, waiting for her body to adjust. After a moment, the slickness between her legs eases my way and the head of my cock pushes past the hint of resistance. I start to thrust deeper, but I don't get far before Libby tenses beneath me. I pause, sensing that something's not right, but before I can ask if she's okay, Libby lifts her hips, taking more of me with a cry that clearly isn't a happy, getting-off sort of sound.

I curse, but I can't resist the instinctive urge to rock my hips forward, driving to the end of her. Libby whimpers in response, and her thighs stiffen against mine, making me feel like absolute shit even as my cock celebrates finally being buried balls-deep in this woman.

I fist my hands in the sheets near her face and clench my jaw, fighting to hold still. All my body wants to do is move, to drive in and out of Libby's tight heat—God, she's tight, so fucking tight—until we both lose our minds with pleasure, but clearly Libby isn't enjoying this. Her eyes are closed, and she's biting her bottom lip, and the warm, pliant woman who welcomed me into her arms is now stiff and guarded, her body language making it clear this isn't nearly as much fun as she thought it would be.

All the signs are there, the signals so clear even an idiot could read them. It normally doesn't take me long to put context clues together and come to logical conclusions, but I'm so positive that Libby would never lie to me that it takes nearly a minute for the truth to penetrate.

"Why didn't you tell me it was your first time, Libs?" I shake my head as her eyes slowly blink open.

"I was going to. But I didn't want to make a big deal out of it." She swallows. "And I guess I was sort of hoping you wouldn't notice?"

"Not notice that you're a virgin?"

Her lips curve in a weak smile. "Well, not anymore…"

My breath rushes out. "What about Brett? You made it sound like you two—"

"I know, but we never did," she says, guilt creeping into her eyes. "We got close. Sort of. But we didn't."

I scowl down at her as I drop my hand to her hip, squeezing her curvy flesh tight as I fight to hold still. Unfortunately, the fact that she misled me is doing nothing to cool my need to pump in and out of the pussy gripping me like a fist. Sweat is breaking out between my shoulders, and my balls are pulsing, demanding I move, but I hold still, refusing to hurt Libby more than I have already.

That's what makes me angry. Not the lie, but that I ended up hurting her because I was in the dark.

"You should have told me," I say. "I could have gone slower. I could have made sure it didn't hurt. Or at least not so much."

"I'm okay," she whispers. "I promise, Jus. It's not that bad."

"I wanted our first time to be a hell of a lot better than not that bad."

"It is." Her fingertips trail down my back to my hips and up again, making my cock twitch inside her. "It's incredible. Even though it stings, it feels so good to have you inside me. I promise."

"And I promise that I'm going to make it feel even better. But I need you to do something for me."

"Anything," she says, with a sincerity that makes my heart do more of that aching, overflowing thing it's been doing since I kissed her in Edna's kitchen. I don't know what I did to deserve to be the first man to make love to her, but I'm going to make this good for her or die trying.

I lean down, pressing my lips to her forehead. "Close your eyes." When she obeys, I whisper against her skin, "Now concentrate on your breath the way we did the other day. Long easy inhalations, and as you exhale imagine the tension leaving your body in little puffs of smoke."

Her eyebrows lift, but her eyes remain closed. "You're serious?"

"Dead serious," I say.

"Is meditation during sex a thing?"

"No, it's not a thing," I say, frustration edging into my tone. "But if you don't relax, I'm going to keep hurting you, Libby, and I hate hurting you. Seriously hate it. So can you just humor me for a minute?"

"Yes, I can." Her fingers skim up my back to my shoulders. "But please don't feel bad. I know you would never hurt me on purpose. You're one of the sweetest, kindest people I know."

"Are you breathing? I don't hear any breathing."

Her lips curve. "I can still tell what you're thinking, you know. Even with my eyes closed. Being sweet and kind isn't something to be embarrassed about."

"I'm not embarrassed, I'm hard." I cup her breast in my hand, brushing my thumb across her nipple. "I'm rock-hard, and I'm buried inside a beautiful woman who won't stop talking and breathe so I can get her relaxed and ready for me to make her come again. It's very frustrating, Libby."

"I thought you liked it when I talked." Her voice hitches as I roll her nipple between my fingers and thumb.

"There's talk and then there's *talk*." I transfer my attention to her other breast, loving the way her lashes flutter against her cheeks in response.

"So if I were talking about how much I love your hands on me, that would be okay?" she asks in a husky voice that makes me think we might not need a meditation session after all.

"That would be acceptable." I kiss her neck, inhaling the heady fragrance of flowers and Libby.

"Or how good it feels when you bite my nipples?"

I rake my teeth over the place where her neck meets her shoulder, and she shivers. "Next time, you can be on top and I'll bite them while you ride me."

"But you should ride me first." She rocks her hips, making me groan as she takes me deeper.

"No pain?" I ask, as I slowly pull back.

"No pain." Her lashes sweep up, giving me a window into her heart again, a window that breaks my heart a little as she whispers, "Can you forgive me?"

"Already forgiven, baby." I glide back into her, breath catching as her body welcomes me in. And for a moment, I want to tell her that I love her.

That I love how her body fits so perfectly against mine and the way her eyes glitter in the semi-darkness, letting me see the exact moment when an absence of pain starts to become an abundance of pleasure. I want to tell her I love the wonder in her expression as I circle her clit with my thumb, coaxing her back to the brink, and the way she reminds me what it was like to make love for the first time—like a miracle, a revelation, a wish coming true with fireworks exploding in the background. I want to tell her that it feels new again for me, too, because I have never made love to someone who is as precious to me as she is, but I force my lips to stay busy kissing her instead.

This isn't the time to talk about feelings and changes of heart and wanting more than sex. But it's hard, so hard that as Libby comes on my cock for the first time, I have to bite the inside of my cheek to keep all the things I shouldn't say from spilling out of my mouth.

"Oh, Justin," she cries out, arms trembling as she pulls me closer. "Oh my God, it's so good. So good, so beautiful."

"Fuck, Libby. Yes, baby." My words end in a groan as I lose myself inside her, my orgasm ripping through me, making my blood run hot and my chest ache. The pleasure is painfully sweet, so close and raw and intimate that when it's over, all I can do is pull Libby close and hug her a little too tight.

I don't want to let her go, but eventually we shift until we're lying side by side on her mattress, and she lifts a tired hand to my face. "Thank you."

"Thank you," I say softly, pressing a kiss to her forehead. "Now get some sleep. But tomorrow we're going to talk. A serious talk. No more lies."

And no more pretending that casual sex is ever going to be enough. I don't want casual. I want it all, every piece of the beautiful person falling to sleep in my arms.

CHAPTER
Twenty-One

Libby

I wake up before the sun and the alarm clock, and do something I haven't done in three years of teaching. I turn off the alarm, swipe my cell from the bedside table, and call in sick.

I'm finishing my message, explaining that I'm running a fever and don't want to come into work in case I'm contagious, when Justin rolls over and his eyes blink open, sending a fluttering, swooping feeling through my stomach, making my voice breathy as I add, "So sorry about this. Please have the sub call me if she needs any help, and tell the kids I'll miss them."

I end the call and set the phone back on the table without breaking eye contact with the scruffy sex god in my bed. He really is a sex god. And last night we really had sex—incredible, intense, multi-orgasmic, life-changing sex—and I am no longer a virgin.

It's all so unexpectedly overwhelming that I'm not sure what to do with myself except stare at Justin and whisper, "Hi."

"Hey." He blinks, squinting against the sun beginning to stream in through my curtains, the slight puffiness around his eyes making him even more handsome.

God, he's beautiful. How on earth did it take me so long to realize that he is the sexiest, best, most wonderful man to ever walk the face of the earth?

Slow your roll there, Collins.

Justin has plenty of flaws, and so do you. Have you forgotten the bumps in the road last night? And how clearly unhappy he was that you fudged the truth?

"You called in sick?" he asks, voice rough with sleep.

"I did. I thought it would be nice not to have to rush that talk."

"Good." His eyes flick down to my shirt before returning to my face. "You got dressed."

"I can't sleep naked."

"Why not?" He pushes up on one arm, sending the sheet slipping down around his waist, low enough for me to see the top of the furry trail that leads to one of my new favorite things in the entire world.

Memories of how it felt to have him inside me, making love to me with a focus and intensity that turned my body to molten lava, shimmy through my thoughts, making my face heat. "Um, I don't know. I just never have. It felt…strange."

"Lots of things are strange at first." He loops his arm around my waist, tugging me toward him so fast I barely have time to yip in surprise before he's on top of me, nudging my legs apart with his thighs. "How are you feeling this morning?"

He pulls up the hem of my oversize sleep shirt and slips his hand down the front of my panties, giving my clitoris a good-morning rub that makes my breath catch before his fingers press gently against where I'm already wet, simply from being this close to him. "Sore?" he asks.

"A little," I confess, "but not as bad as I thought I would be. Actually, I…"

"Yes?" He slides a single finger inside me, a decision my body welcomes with a shiver and a rush of heat between my legs.

"I sort of wish…" I press my lips together, swallowing hard as he adds a second finger, stretching me until I'm more aware of the lingering tenderness, but equally aware of how much my body wants this. Wants *him*.

"What do you wish, Libby?" He kisses my cheek and then my neck, his breath warm on my throat. "I want you to tell me, beautiful. Tell me what you want."

"I want you," I whisper, running my hands down the strong expanse of his back, marveling that this powerful man can be so perfectly gentle when he needs to be. "I want you inside me again."

"Are you sure?" He captures my fingers, guiding them between us to where he's already hot and hard.

I wrap my hand around him, squeezing gently. "Trying to remind me how big and scary it is?" I ask, smiling as his cock pulses in my hand in response.

"I wouldn't say scary…" His free hand slides up my shirt, cupping my breast, making me arch into his touch as I continue to stroke him, summoning that fluid that pearls at the tip of him when he wants me.

"It was scary before I knew we would fit," I confess, amazed all over again at how quickly he brings my body to life, and how heady it is to know I'm doing the same to him. "I was afraid you were going to rip through my vagina like a tornado through a trailer park."

He snorts and quickly turns his face away from mine. "Don't make me laugh. I'm trying not to breathe on you until I get a chance to brush my teeth. I don't want to scare you away with my morning breath."

"I'm not scared of your breath." I spread my legs wider, guiding the tip of him to where I ache.

"Let me get a condom," he says, but I stop him with a hand on his face.

"I'm on the pill. And I'm clean. So as long as you are…"

"I am." His eyes blaze into mine, making me

even more keenly aware of how close we are to coming together, and how much I need him to fill the emptiness inside me, an emptiness I didn't know was there until he showed me what it felt like to be so satisfied, so complete. "But I haven't had sex without a condom in years, Libs. I can't promise I'll last as long as I did last night."

"That's okay." My heart beats faster as his hips pulse forward, pressing the head of his cock lightly against me. "I just want to know what it feels like without something in between. When it's just you and me."

"Just you and me," he echoes softly as he cups my bottom in his hands, tilting my hips toward him. And then he pushes forward, gliding inside me with one slow, sure thrust that makes lights flash behind my eyes as they slide closed.

My arms tremble as they wrap around him, holding him close as my body adjusts to the sweet invasion. It only takes a moment this time, a breath of discomfort that's quickly banished by the waves of pleasure pulsing through my inner walls as they grip him tight, celebrating his return.

"Not too sore?" he asks, nipping the lobe of my ear as his hand returns to my breast, teasing and plucking my nipple as he holds still deep inside of me.

"No. It's good. So good." My eyes flutter open as I skim my palms down the small of his back to cup his ass. "Even better than last night. I love that I can feel how hot your skin is."

"I love feeling how wet you are for me." He circles his hips, grinding against me while pulling out, sending his pubic bone rolling over my clit, making my pulse spike. "But I want you even wetter." He guides my leg up and around his hips. "Move with me, baby," he says, urging me closer. "Show me how you want it."

"Like this." I nudge him with my hips, silently telling him to move a little faster.

Faster, faster....

But not that fast.

A little slower and...*there*. There. That's it... Oh God, that's it...

I roll against him, my entire body getting into the act, pressing my breasts to his chest and then my hips tight to his, the tension and the need to have him thrusting inside building as my pussy squeezes him tight.

Tighter...

Tighter, until the line snaps and pleasure crashes through me, devastating my body with bliss so beautiful the only way to survive it is to cling to Justin, crying out his name as he finally begins to drive inside me.

He pulls out and plunges back in, groaning against my neck as I wrap my legs around his waist and hold on for dear life. "God, Libby, you're still so tight. Am I hurting you, baby?"

"No," I promise, gasping as his next thrust sends him even deeper, so deep I feel him everywhere, in every pulsing, throbbing cell in my body. I drag my teeth over his skin, biting into his muscled shoulder, a choice that, judging by the way he growls in response, is one Justin approves of.

"Fuck, Libby." His voice is as rough as the hand he fists in my hair, holding me captive as he kisses and bites my neck and his thrusts come harder, faster, deeper. "I'm in love with your pussy. I want to own this sweet pussy every night, every morning."

I cry out, rocking into him as the tension begins to build again, swelling between my hips and spinning through my head.

"I want to be buried inside you every fucking chance I can get." He pinches my nipple between his fingers, but it doesn't hurt. It only makes the heavy, hungry, desperate feeling swell bigger and bigger, until I'm clawing at Justin's shoulders as we chase after what we both need.

And then suddenly, I'm back at the razor's edge and pleasure slices through me, making me scream, a raw, primal sound that echoes through the room as Justin groans against my throat. His hand grips my hip tight, as his rhythm grows erratic and his cock pistons between my legs, driving in and out of where I'm still coming, my inner walls clutching at him every time he pulls out. "Yes, baby. I love feeling you come on my cock."

I cry out something in response, but I have no idea what. I am beyond language, beyond words, spinning in a world of heat and pleasure and animal bliss, my orgasm spiraling on for so long that I'm still pulsing when Justin loses himself a moment later. His cock jerks hard, again and again, his release rushing inside me, making the last few seconds of my flight even sweeter because I get to share it with him.

To be lost with him. Found with him. To be held tight while this powerful, impressively put together man melts in my arms because he's as devastated by the beauty we make together as I am.

After, he lies heavily on top of me, and I run my fingers slowly through his hair, wishing we could stay just like this for the rest of the day, with our hearts pounding in time and nothing separating me from the person I love except our sweat-damp skin.

My hand stills in his hair and my eyes squeeze closed.

There it is again. The L word. It's just a thought for now, but I know better than to think I can keep it hidden for long. Sooner or later, Justin is going to see the truth written all over my face.

He's going to see that I broke the rules and fell in love with him.

"Now we need to talk." His breath—which isn't dragony at all, proving he really is exceptional in every way—stirs the hair on my forehead. "I think we both know this isn't working out the way we thought it would, Libs."

I bite my bottom lip as a wave of sadness washes through me, cooling the warm, happy, post-orgasm glow. Suddenly I feel like I'm going to cry, proving I'm not emotionally equipped to have this conversation right now, especially not while he's still softening inside of me.

I'm about to tell Justin that I need to take a shower and get dressed—preferably in a suit of armor—before we talk, when the sound of the front door slamming echoes through my tiny apartment and my sister calls out in a chipper voice, "Hey babes. You want to grab coffee and donuts before you head to work? I got up early and thought we could TGIF it over at Buddy's."

Justin and I lock eyes with twin expressions of horror.

"Fuck," he whispers at the same moment that I hiss, "Shit!"

A moment later, we vault out of bed and start tossing clothes at each other from the floor, scrambling to get dressed before Laura barges in to my bedroom and discovers just how "friendly" Justin and I have been getting behind her back.

CHAPTER
Twenty-Two

Justin

I've managed to get my boxer briefs and jeans on, and am struggling into my tee shirt when Libby whispers, "Get down!" and gives my arm a sharp tug. I drop onto my belly between the bed and the window seconds before her bedroom door opens.

"Hey, what's up?" Laura hums beneath her breath before she continues in a concerned tone, "Are you okay? I thought you'd be dressed by now."

"I called in sick to work," Libby says, sounding way too breathless for a woman who just rolled out of bed.

"Oh. Are you sick? You don't look sick."

"No, I feel fine." Libby crosses her arms at her chest and moves to the foot of the bed, hopefully blocking Laura's progress into the room.

If she gets much closer, she's going to see me doing my best impression of a throw rug over here on the floor. For a moment, I consider scooting under the bed, but I'm not sure I'll fit and there's a significant chance that I'll make a noise that Libby won't be able to explain away.

"I just felt like taking a day off," Libby says with a shrug.

Laura snorts. "What? Are you serious?"

"Can't a girl take a mental health day now and then? You're the one who's always telling me that I need to practice self-care."

"Yes, but you never listen," Laura says as the mattress springs groan, making me think she must have sat down on the bed, probably mere feet from the tangle of covers where I was banging her sister a few minutes ago.

I squeeze my eyes shut, bracing myself for the moment when Laura catches a whiff of Eau de Recently Been Laid and realizes her little sister must be hiding a man somewhere in her room.

Instead, the mattress squeaks again as Libby lunges forward.

"Well, I'm listening now." Libby hauls Laura up and out of the room, her voice growing distant as she adds, "So why don't you make some coffee while I get dressed. And then we can go get donuts and hang out until you have to go to work."

I wait until I hear Laura murmuring her response from somewhere deeper in the apartment and then launch back into motion. By the time Libby returns, slamming the door and locking it behind her, I'm dressed and pulling on my shoes.

"Give me ten minutes, and I'll have her out of here," she says, whipping off her sleep shirt and throwing it to the floor, granting me a truly heart-stopping view of her in pink panties and nothing else before she grabs her bra from the floor and slips it on. "Then you can escape without being spotted."

"Or you could tell Laura you've decided you would rather sleep late and stay here." I watch her hook her bra, my cock appreciating the view of her breasts arched forward so much it thickens in my jeans, insisting its ready for morning sex, round two. "I'll stay with you, and we can take a long, hot shower."

She casts me an odd look, as if she isn't quite sure what I mean by long, hot shower—I mean a shower that involves me washing her clean and then getting her dirty again, of course—and then shakes her head. "I can't. She's already suspicious because I called in sick without actually being sick. If I change my mind about hanging out two minutes after promising her donuts, she'll know something's up."

"I thought women were entitled to change their minds."

"Not me. I'm not the mind-changer in the family. You know that." She shrugs on a pink sweatshirt and the brown linen pants from last night, quickly covering all her delectable parts. "I'm the dependable one who is on time for work, never cheats on her taxes, and is always up for sisterly bonding activities."

"All right," I say, since it's clear her mind is made up. "Then text me later? I'm free until practice tonight. I can swing by anytime. I want to finish the talk we barely got started."

"Okay," she says, but she doesn't sound any more thrilled about talking than she did before we were so rudely interrupted. "Thanks for a wonderful morning. And a wonderful night." She slips into my arms, hugging me tight, making me realize all over again how much I want to keep holding her, making love to her, waking up next to her as something more than a friend.

But before I can tell her that it was wonderful for me, too, and that I can't wait for another wonderful night tonight—assuming she'll consent to having me shack up with her two nights in a row—she pulls away and heads for the bathroom.

"I should hurry. Laura's not known for her patience," she mumbles, shutting the door behind her.

While the water runs in the bathroom, I make Libby's bed and arrange the decorative pillows artistically, keeping busy as I mull over what she said.

It's true, Libby isn't known for changing her mind. She knew she was going to be a teacher from the time she was in kindergarten herself, decided she loved dressing like a gypsy and embraced the look fully by the time she was twelve, and still spends hours volunteering for the same causes she's been passionate about since she organized her first knit-in for the ASPCA in high school. She's open to trying new things, but once she finds something that works, Libby's not one to mess with a formula or flip the script.

Clearly the friends-with-benefits situation is working fine as far as she's concerned. Maybe she doesn't want to talk because she doesn't want to fix something that, in her opinion, isn't broken.

Or maybe she doesn't want to talk because she can tell you're wading into the deep end of the emotion pool, and she's dreading breaking the news that she's going to let you drown out there alone.

You know Libby. She hates to hurt people's feelings, especially people she considers friends.

Friends. Fuck friends.

I don't want to be friends, and as I wait for Libby to get out of the bathroom, I start plotting ways to convince her that she doesn't want to just be friends, either.

I'll show her that we're better off as something more, that this isn't the kind of thing you let slip through your fingers without a fight. I've never had such an instant, powerful connection to a lover, and I can't remember the last time I came as hard as I did this morning, with Libby's sweet smell filling my head and the molten heat of her pussy locked tight around my cock. And it's not just the sex; it's how good it feels to share the day with Libby, to hear her thoughts, see her smile, and be there to kiss her hard when the assholes of the world are bringing her down. It's the way that it doesn't matter if we're at my place or hers—as long as Libby's with me, I feel like I'm at home.

We're good together, good for each other, and one way or another I'm going to bring her around to my way of thinking.

I'm imagining all the sexy, romantic, orgasm-inducing arguments I'll make to win Libby over to the more-than-friends side of the fence when the lock on the bedroom door pops with a sharp snap and the door slams open. And there, fuming in the doorway, is Laura, my messenger bag over her arm, my keys in one hand, and the Allen wrench she used to break into Libby's bedroom in the other.

"I knew it!" she shouts, pointing an accusing finger at my chest. "I knew it smelled like your cologne in here, you bastard. What the hell are you doing putting your dick in my little sister?"

CHAPTER
Twenty-Three

Libby

My protective, loving big sis is good at many things, but calm conflict resolution is not one of them. She got the Irish temper to go along with her red hair and freckles, and she got it in spades.

The moment I hear her start to lay into Justin, I know the only chance of this ending without bloodshed is if I can distract Laura long enough for Justin to escape out the front door. She won't be capable of talking this through with him until her blood pressure drops—sometime in the next two to three days. Or months. Or maybe years, if the volume of her current screeching is anything to judge by.

I drop my hairbrush in the sink and bolt out of the bathroom, hurling myself between Laura and Justin seconds before shouting becomes something more violent.

"Get out of the way, Libby." Laura glares at Justin over my head, enough heat in her gaze to set Justin's eyebrows on fire. "I need to kick this selfish son of a bitch's ass."

"Laura, please," Justin says, "you don't understand, I—"

"Oh, I understand just fine, asshole," Laura says at the same time that I shout, "Just get out of here, Justin. Go home. I'll call you later."

"I'm not running away from this." He stands up straighter, shaking his head. "There's no reason we can't sit down and talk like grownups."

"Do you know me?" Laura screeches, making my argument for me. "Have we fucking met? Because if you think I'm going to sit down and calmly fucking discuss how it's okay for you to use Libby as your rebound fuck because you're too lazy not to shit where you eat, then I'm beginning to seriously doubt we were ever actually friends, Justin Cruise."

"Please, just go." I block Laura as she lunges to the left, trying to get around me. "Go, Justin! Now! Staying isn't helping. I promise I'll call you later."

"Fine." He circles around where I'm grappling with Laura, doing my best to keep her from scratching Justin's eyes out as he passes by and snatches his bag and keys from the floor by the door. "But this isn't what you think it is, Laura. And honestly, it's none of your damned business.

Libby and I are both grownups."

"I'm going to show you how grown up you are," Laura shouts after him as he heads for the front door, her face flushing a deep, angry, only-possible-for-the-Irish shade of red. "The next time I see you I'm going to kick your ass, Justin! The same way I kicked your ass in tenth grade when you slept with Miranda!"

I blink up at her, my grip on her wrists loosening as the front door slams shut, signaling Justin's successful escape. "He slept with Miranda? Your best friend Miranda?"

"Yes. He did." Laura pulls out of my grasp and points an accusing finger toward the front of the apartment. "And he did it after I *begged* him not to mess with my friends. But he went ahead and did it anyway. It was at a Halloween party, when they both ended up sleeping over in Tim Holler's basement. For Justin, it was just another one-night stand, no big deal, but Miranda had feelings for him. She was so embarrassed to see his stupid face that she refused to set foot in our neighborhood, let alone the house right next door to his."

"I remember she stopped coming over," I say, a knot forming in my stomach. "But I didn't know why."

"That fucking jerk is why." Laura paces out of my bedroom and into the living room, crossing to the windows overlooking the street. "Losing friends was one of the major downsides of living next door to a boy-whore who cared more about getting his dick serviced than who he was hurting in the process." She pauses, wrenching up the window with a sharp jerk before shouting through the screen, "That's right! Keep walking, asshole! And don't you fucking look back. Because I swear to God, Justin, I am going to kill you for this."

"Shut the window." I hurry around her, pulling the pane down and blocking her attempt to pull it back up again. "Seriously, Laura, stop! Two other teachers from my school live in the building. On the off chance that they haven't heard all the cussing and shouting coming from this apartment when I'm supposed to be home sick, please put a lid on it!"

Laura's breath rushes out and a moment later she sinks to the floor beside the window, leaning back against the wall as she looks up at me with a pained expression. "Shit. I'm sorry, Libby."

"It's okay," I say, grateful that the anger storm seems to be abating. "I know you have a temper, La. It's nothing new."

"No, I'm not sorry about that," she says, scowling darkly. "I'm sorry that I let this happen. I knew Justin would be on the rebound, but I never imagined that he would go after you. I thought he had more respect for our family and our friendship than that." She shakes her head sadly. "But that's no excuse. I should have paid attention. I should have seen what was happening and protected you."

I run a hand through my hair. "That's sweet, Laura, but I don't need you to protect me. Especially not from Justin."

"You say that because you don't know how he is." She lays her palm flat on her chest. "But I've had a front row seat to every single one of his relationships for the past four years. He does the same thing every time, Libby. He breaks up with a girl he's been serious with for a few months and immediately jumps into bed with the next woman who will hold still long enough for him to get his dick out of his pants."

I roll my eyes. "That's not what—"

"All while vehemently protesting that it isn't a rebound and that he has real feelings for this woman," Laura barrels on, jabbing her finger into the carpet beneath her for emphasis. "And then, like clockwork, a few weeks later, he breaks it off with the rebound girl, says he's sick of the drama and is never going to date again, and starts one of those crazy giant afghan projects that takes hundreds of hours to finish. All of this, of course, is to avoid feeling shitty about the end of the relationship he actually did care about, which is never the relationship with the rebound girl. The rebound girl is just Kleenex, Libs, tissue to mop up some of the emotional mess before being thrown away."

I sink to the floor beside her, sitting cross-legged on the carpet, not enjoying the ugly, stomach-twisting, you've-been-played feeling rising inside me. It's a ridiculous way to feel. I haven't been played. It isn't Justin's fault that I let my heart get involved in what we agreed would be a no-strings relationship. I knew what I was getting into from the start.

Did you really?

You wanted dating and sex advice. You didn't go into this wanting to kiss Justin, let alone sleep with him. And if you hadn't slept together, chances are you wouldn't have suddenly decided that you have romantic feelings for a person you've been friends with for over a decade.

I swallow past the lump in my throat and ignore the inner voice. I can't afford to get upset about this now. If I do, that will be all the confirmation Laura needs that she's obligated to get revenge on Justin on my behalf, and my sister on the revenge warpath is a scary thing to behold.

"I hear you," I say gently. "But that's not what's going on with Justin and me. I asked him to do this."

Laura's auburn brows lift. "You asked him to go out with you? But what about Roger? I thought he was the one you were crazy about."

"He is," I say, though I'm not sure that's the truth anymore. I'm not sure of anything except that I need to get Laura calmed down and headed for work so I can give myself some time to process the events of the past twenty-four hours. "But you know how shy I am around men I like. That's why I asked Justin for help. We were never dating, we were just…"

"Banging like bunnies?" Laura's bewildered expression makes it clear she isn't buying what I'm selling. "But Libby, that's so not you."

I hold my hands up, fingers spread wide. "You're right. It's not. But I'm tired of being shy, anxious, hasn't-had-a-date-in-years Libby. I want to be confident and sure of myself, and being with Justin has helped with that. He wasn't using me. We were using each other." I shrug as I glance down at my folded legs, remembering what Jus said that first day in the woods when we decided to go for a more hands-on approach to my education. "He even mentioned the rebound problem, and said he was glad we were doing the friends-with-benefits thing so he wouldn't end up rebounding after the breakup with Sylvia."

Laura is quiet for so long that I finally look up, meeting her scowl with a stiff smile. "I'm serious, La. That's what happened. Justin and I made this decision together. Eyes open, heads clear. I'm fine. You don't need to beat him up, and we can all go back to being friends like we've always been. Like he said, we're all grownups."

She shakes her head slowly. "And you really believe that?"

"I do," I say, anger prickling through the other confusing emotions swirling in my chest. I might be inexperienced, but I'm not a fool. Justin didn't betray me, I betrayed myself by letting my stupid, squishy heart get attached to him in a way I shouldn't have.

"Okay," Laura says in a tone that makes it clear it's not okay at all, "but I saw the way you looked at him while he was running out of here like a coward, Libby. And it wasn't anything like the way you usually look at him."

I stretch my neck to one side, rubbing the tight muscles with my fingers. "Yeah, well, I'm not usually worried that you're going to draw first blood in my bedroom, either," I say, doing my best to deflect attention from my change of heart where Justin is concerned. "I haven't seen you that angry in years. I kind of thought you'd outgrown the crazy rage-spiral."

"Well, I haven't." She crosses her arms tightly over her chest. "And it wasn't a crazy rage-spiral; it was a completely justified rage-spiral. Because I love you and I don't want to see you get your heart broken." Her shoulders lift and fall. "And selfishly, I wanted things to stay the way they've always been. I wanted to keep being Justin's friend and not have to hate him for hurting my sister. I don't like having to choose sides and lose someone who's important to me."

"You won't have to choose sides." I lay my hand on her knee, giving it a squeeze. "I promise. Even if Justin and I made a mistake and this experiment doesn't end well, it will be okay. I've been friends with him almost half my life, La. We're going to still be friends when the other stuff is over."

Though, I really don't want to think about the other stuff being over, not when I've just discovered how beautiful and perfect and right sex can feel. But the cold, hard fact remains that once Justin and I have our "talk" I'll probably never be with him again. I'm a terrible liar, and I wouldn't want to lie about this anyway. If he asks if I'm having more-than-friends feelings for him, I'm going to tell him the truth. And chances are he'll tell me that he's out.

"I hope that's true," Laura says softly. "But in my experience, it isn't easy to go back to being friends after sex enters the picture. Especially if you aren't the one who decides he would rather not sleep with you anymore."

"Who decided he would rather not sleep with you?" I tip my head, but Laura refuses to meet my eyes. "Not Henry. I thought you said you broke things off with him after you caught him trying on your underwear."

Laura snorts. "God, that was a weird morning. Yeah, I definitely called it off with him. I'm not up for sharing my underwear with anyone, male or female. Panties are sacred. They're the guardians of crotch secrets, you know?"

My lips curve. "That's how I always think of them—as the guardians of my crotch secrets."

"Right?" She laughs, but her smile fades as she takes my hand. "No, it was another guy. We'd been friends for a while. Then one night we ended up hooking up at this party. It was…really nice."

"But…"

"But his life is complicated, and he decided there wasn't room for me in it, and that was that." She sighs. "And it's been weird ever since. Every time I see him, I can't help but think about how easy it was for him to tell me thanks, but no thanks, and I wonder if maybe I'm the worst lay on the planet. Or maybe I'm just unlikable or untrustworthy or generally not good enough for this very serious, very great guy who I think the world of. And that's a crappy feeling. And we're definitely not friends anymore. Not the way we used to be."

I squeeze her fingers. "You are very likeable, as well as one of the most generous and trustworthy people I know. And I'm sure your vagina is dynamite."

She wrinkles her nose. "You're so gross. You know I really and truly hate that word, right? It's not just something I complain about so we can laugh about it later. It's like acid is being poured into my ears."

I grin. "I know. I enjoy making you cringe. It's a simple pleasure."

"You're more sadistic than people give you credit for," she says, nudging my foot with hers. "There's a dark soul hidden inside that cute kindergarten-teacher body."

"Totally dark," I agree, nudging her back. "But seriously, whoever this guy is, it's his loss. You're

LILI VALENTE

a great catch and a good person."

"Thanks." She presses her lips together, wiggling them back and forth before she adds in a conciliatory tone, "And maybe I'm wrong. Maybe it will be different for you and Justin. Maybe it will be easy to go back to being friends."

"I hope so," I say, but the more I think about it, the more I worry that Laura is right.

Am I ever going to be able to look at Justin without thinking about last night and this morning and how incredible it felt to be so connected to him? And not just physically, but emotionally. Making love to him is the most intimate thing that's ever happened to me, and it's quickly becoming the most terrifying. I feel so vulnerable, so exposed and defenseless, that by the time I get Laura off to work and settle down to text Justin, I can't figure out what to say.

I sit huddled under a fleece blanket on the couch, scrolling back through our old messages, rereading the silly poem Justin wrote for me until I have it memorized, my thoughts turning in restless circles. Finally, I drop the phone on the coffee table and jump into the shower, hoping the warm water will clear my head.

But my tender nipples, lightly whisker-burned cheeks, and the soreness between my legs keep reminding me that everything has changed and I have no idea what to do about it. I emerge from the bathroom twenty minutes later as confused as when I went in, and discover a string of text

230

messages from Justin waiting on my phone—

Hey, Brendan called a few minutes ago. Chloe started running a fever at school, her babysitter isn't available until three, and Brendan is two hours away filming a commercial. So I said I would go pick Chloe up, take her home, and watch movies with her until the sitter gets there this afternoon.

I'll have to go straight to practice after, but I can come to your place when I'm done. I'd rather not wait until nine o'clock at night to talk, but I don't want to do this over the phone. I think it's better if we talk in person.

I'm assuming you've got Laura under control by now. I'm sorry you had to deal with that alone. I'll give her a couple of days to cool off, and then I'll smooth things over. Once she understands the situation, I'm hoping she won't want to kill me anymore.

Maybe just maim me a little. Cut off a finger or harvest an organ or something.

Anyway…

I miss you already.

Enjoy your day off, beautiful. Do something fun. I'll be thinking about you.

The messages send a wave of happy sadness spreading through my chest, mixed with a healthy dose of confusion. My gut says these aren't the texts of a man who's planning to break things off with his friend-with-benefits, but my brain cautions that Justin wanting to talk face-to-face doesn't bode well, and meanwhile, my heart runs around in frantic circles insisting that we should all jump into my car and drive to meet Justin at

Brendan's house right now because an entire day is too long to wait to confess the way we feel.

I haven't felt this conflicted or confused since the day my mother told me she'd decided it was time to stop homeschooling and for me to join the rest of the kids at our local high school. She'd been happy to be home with me, but she needed to go back to work, and felt that the public school would do a better job of preparing me for college.

I'd been terrified, but excited. Eager to expand my social circle to people outside the group of friends who lived on our street, and simultaneously certain that I would never fit in with normal kids who hadn't been born with a stutter, higher than average anxiety levels, and a tendency to babble inanely when they were nervous. The only thing that kept me from having a panic attack the first day was that I got to ride to CHS in Justin's car, with my big sister and my friend in the front seat. By that point, Justin and I had been crochet buddies for years and he felt almost like family. Knowing that at least two people at my new school loved me and believed I could handle freshman year had made all the difference.

Looking back on the past decade-plus of friendship, Justin has been there for me more times than I can count. And I've done the same for him. When he was in meltdown mode his rookie season, it wasn't Laura he turned to for help, it was me. Because we've always had a special connection, a quiet, solid friendship that isn't as flashy or flamboyant as his wild weekends with my sister and their mutual friends, but is every bit as real. He is one of the touchstones in my life, a person I've always known I could trust to have my back and to give it to me straight when I need real advice, not meaningless platitudes.

And now I've put that at risk. Put *us* at risk.

How did I ever think this was a good idea? How stupid was I to fool myself into thinking that having sex wasn't going to change things between us forever?

Even a dumb virgin should have known better, but I didn't, and now I feel so lost. I can't talk to Laura, that's for damned sure, and I can't talk to Justin, either, at least not until I untangle all the things I'm feeling. And that isn't going to happen by nine o'clock tonight.

Finally certain about something, I text back—
I'll be thinking about you, too, but I can't talk tonight. Or tomorrow really. I have to get up early to volunteer at the animal shelter, and then I've got lesson plans to put together for next week.

I think we should wait and talk after the game tomorrow night. Just seems like better timing.

Better timing for getting my heart torn into a hundred soggy, sad little pieces.

As if there's ever going to be a good time for that. But at least Justin won't be distracted by my messy emotions while he's trying to focus on the game. I know him. If he has to hurt me, it's going to hurt him, and no amount of meditation will be able to get him back on track if he's lost a friend less than twenty-four hours before hitting the ice.

And it will be a friendship lost, I'm afraid. I don't see a way back to where we were from here. I can't imagine being in the same room with Justin and not wanting to touch him, kiss him, or see him smile in that way that I know is just for me.

Maybe I can get out practice. The message pops up on my screen, followed quickly by, *Shit, no, I can't. Coach is shuffling the lines. I need to be there.*

I text back, *It's okay. Tomorrow night is good. That way you can focus on the game and we can take our time talking things through after.*

All right. But remember your promise. If I don't see some quality Sext Goddess action on my phone after the game, I'll know who's to blame for the break in the Badgers winning streak.

I nibble my lip, not sure I'll be able to work my sexting magic while I'm this uncertain about what the future holds for Justin and me, but nevertheless I type, *The Sext Goddess will be on her best—or rather, worst—behavior. And you're not going to lose. Think positive thoughts.*

You, too. And think some thoughts about my cock while you're at it. He's going to miss you tonight…

"I'll miss him, too," I whisper aloud, my cozy apartment feeling cold and empty for the first time since I moved in right out of college.

I've always been the kind of person who thrives on solitude—I need it to focus, recharge, and get ready to tackle the world outside my door—but right now I would happily handcuff myself to Justin and throw away the key if there were any way to make a conjoined lifestyle work. If the school didn't frown on bringing significant others to work, or if I could skate half as well as I ski.

Which is as much reason as any to take at least a day to think about what's going on here. I don't want to become one of those people who can't function without her boyfriend around, especially considering Justin *isn't* my boyfriend and might not even be my fuck buddy for much longer.

My phone dings again, but when I glance down, the text isn't from Justin. It's Bethany, whose first-grade classroom is right across the hall from mine. *So sorry to hear you're sick! Especially today. A bunch of us are going to the tapas place you like for happy hour after school. I was going to ask you to come!*

Happy hour. With Bethany, other teachers, and no one who knows about my current drama. It sounds like a little piece of heaven, so I text back, *I'm actually feeling better already. I was just a little off when I woke up this morning.*

*Oh good! Then you should come. We're meeting at 4:30. And don't worry, Principal Edwards won't be there, so your miraculous recovery from your "sick" day can stay our secret *winking face emoji**

I smile, though I'm not terribly worried about Principal Edwards. She knows I work harder than all three of the other kindergarten teachers put together. Unfortunately for the rest of the six-year-olds at Asher Elementary, Mr. Vickers, Mrs. Gray, and Miss Thompson are all various levels of exhausted and/or ready to move on to teaching kids with fewer potty emergencies. I am Edwards' top performer for five- and six-year-olds, and I seriously doubt she would reprimand me for taking a personal day.

I text Bethany again, telling her I'll see her this afternoon, and then scroll through the movie listings, buying a ticket to a noon showing of an action flick. I'll do some thinking this morning, let myself be distracted by things getting blown up on the big screen, do some more thinking, and then do my best to leave sex and romance worries behind and enjoy an evening with friends.

It's a good plan, and by the time I find a parking spot near the tapas place, I've decided what I'll say to Justin when the time comes, marveled at how many explosions can be squished into a ninety-minute feature film, and managed to convince Laura via text to leave work early so there won't be the slightest chance of her crossing paths with Justin again today.

I'm feeling pretty good—nervous, but proud of myself for taking time to think at least semi-rationally about all the things I'm feeling—when I swing into El Toro and realize I've made a mistake assuming happy hour would be a safe space.

It's not. Bethany, Rebecca, and the rest of the south-wing crew aren't here alone. They've brought a member of administration along.

Roger sits at the head of the long table, in the only chair with an unobstructed view of the entrance. The moment I spy him, he spies me— lifting a friendly hand in hello, dashing all hopes of making a quick getaway.

Silently cursing my luck, I force a smile, praying I'll be able to make it through a happy hour beverage without falling flat on my face or doing something else clumsy, awkward, or embarrassing. I'm not sure what I feel for Roger at this point—it's hard to think about anything but Justin—but if anyone could manage to make a fool of herself over someone she isn't even interested in anymore, it'd be yours truly.

CHAPTER
Twenty-Four

Libby

Nothing. Absolutely nothing.

That's what I feel when Bethany springs out of her seat next to Roger and deftly settles me into her place, making it clear at least one of my coworkers is aware that I have the hots for the VP.

Or that I *had* the hots for him.

Now that I know what it feels like to experience real passion and pleasure and an intimate, heart-stopping connection to another person, I realize that what I felt for Roger was never "the hots." It wasn't lust or love or anything close to what I feel for Jus. It was a crush, a fixation based on fantasy spawned by the fact that before Roger carried me to the nurse's office, I'd never had anything remotely romantic happen to me.

But now I've had poetry and stolen kisses in the woods and in an elevator and behind Edna's bushes. I've had sexts and flirting that feels as natural as breathing and more orgasms then I can count on two hands.

I've had Justin, who calls me beautiful and makes me believe I am, every time we touch. But when Roger says he's glad I could make it to happy hour, I feel nothing except grateful that I'll never have to be nervous around this poor man again.

"Thank you." I smile as I pluck a menu from the center of the table. "So are we ordering food to share? Or fending for ourselves? I had popcorn an hour ago, but I'm already starving."

An hour later, I've shared Octopus a la Plancha and Jamon Croquettes with Bethany, an order of Radicchio Toast with Rebecca, and a mini cheese board with Roger, all while carrying on easy, pleasant conversation about school, life, and Thanksgiving plans. There isn't a single moment of awkwardness, not even when my fingers brush Roger's as we're both reaching for a slice of Manchego.

I simply draw my hand away, waiting until he's made his choice, and then dart back in for the kill. I've already eaten enough to fill me up on a normal day, but for some reason I'm still starving.

Maybe it's all the sex, I think, cheeks flushing as I wonder how many calories Justin and I burned in the past twenty-four hours and if it's enough to justify an order of mandarin panna cotta.

"You should take a personal day more often," Roger says, tapping the table beside my plate lightly with two fingers. "Relaxed looks good on you."

"Thanks," I say with a laugh. "Though Principal Edwards probably wouldn't appreciate me playing hooky on a regular basis."

He smiles, and I silently acknowledge that he is still a very decent, clean, friendly-looking person. But he's not Justin. His smile doesn't make my belly flutter or my chest ache, and his compliment, while nice to receive, is just that— nice. The world hasn't shifted on its axis, no secrets of the heart have been revealed, and when my leg brushes against his knee as I sneak out to head to the bathroom, I'm not flustered at all.

It isn't until I swing out of the last stall and step up to the row of sinks to wash my hands that I experience a moment of panic.

There, right beside me, is none other than Sylvia.

Justin's Sylvia. Or the one who used to be Justin's Sylvia…

I duck my head, hoping she won't notice me or recognize my face if she does—we only met a few times, and I've found truly stunning people like Sylvia tend to forget the names of less stunning people like me—but once again I'm out of luck. She squeaks in surprise as she shuts off the water and reaches for a towel from the dispenser between us.

"Hey, there! Libby, right? Justin's friend?"

I nod, grinning with my lips closed because I probably have something in my teeth. I was going to check as soon as I washed my hands, but now I can't because I have to try to have a normal conversation while standing next to a woman who used to have sex with the only man I've ever had sex with. The man who this very morning was inside me, but was probably inside *her* only a week or two previously.

And though I realize this is something that the average nearly-twenty-five-year-old wouldn't stress about, it strikes me as profoundly, disturbingly strange. So strange, it takes me several awkward moments to convince my mouth to form the words, "Yes. That's me. How are you, Sylvia?"

"Oh, as well as can be expected," she says with a sigh, leaning her slim hip against the sink as she dries her hands. She's wearing a clingy red dress that perfectly showcases her model tall, model thin body, and her olive skin seems to gleam like a beautiful piece of freshly polished furniture. "Breakups are the worst, but it will all work out for the best in the end."

I nod with a little too much enthusiasm in an attempt to look like an innocent person who isn't sleeping with her ex. "Right. Totally. Well—"

"It's the living situation that's the hardest," she pushes on before I can excuse myself and dash for the door. "I mean, we'd just moved in together, but I'd already given up my apartment."

I wince. "That was jerky of him. To kick you out like that."

They're traitorous words, but they're true. Justin can be a jerk sometimes, especially when it comes time to say good-bye. He doesn't think, he just takes action and worries about the fallout when pieces of debris start pelting his head. I know this about him, and it's one of the things I thought about today when I was doing my best to remember that he isn't a beautiful, perfect, sweet, thoughtful sex god all the time.

Sylvia huffs and rolls her eyes again. "Tell me about it. I mean, I know he's been your friend forever, and I don't want to put you in the middle of anything, but it was a pain in the ass finding a place to crash. I ended up on my friend Casey's couch." She waves an elegant hand breezily through the air. "But it's fine. She doesn't care if my boxes are stacked against her wall for a few weeks while Justin works through his issues and realizes he's made a mistake."

My mouth goes dry and I can't think of a single thing to say aside from things I absolutely can't say, like he's never going to realize he made a mistake, Sylvia, because he's with me now, and he's mine, and I licked him and peed on him—in the metaphorical sense, not the literal sense, because that would be disgusting. I'm saying that I've marked Justin as my territory and that's it's over, super model girl, no sharing, no take backs. Mine, mine, and also, mine.

But it's okay that I'm tongue-tied because Sylvia has plenty to say.

"He's called me twice already," she says with a silly, secret smile, one that is innocently happy, not vicious, because she clearly has no idea that Justin and I are more than friends. "Today he said he was calling to make sure I didn't need my bike from the storage unit in his building before Sunday because he was going to be busy this weekend, but we ended up talking for almost an hour. It was nice. We cut through a lot of the bullshit. Got real, you know?"

I swallow hard and manage to convince my head to bob up and down a couple of times.

Justin talked to her today. *Today*, after he left *my* bed and texted *me*, wanting to get together and talk, he called and chatted with Sylvia instead. For an hour. And they "got real," whatever that means.

It could mean anything. Or nothing.

He has her bike and they just broke up and they have normal, just-broken-up things to talk about.

"It was so nice to hear him say that he realizes that he wasn't giving as much to our relationship as he should have been. As much as I deserved." Her gaze is soft, unfocused, as if she's reliving the moment Justin made it clear that he's on his way back to her, sooner or later.

He's on his way back to her. He really is.

Why else would he have called her and said all of those things?

Why else except that sleeping with someone he wasn't in love with showed him that he wants something more, something meaningful and romantic with a beautiful, confident, successful woman? It's just like Laura said. The rebound girl is just a phase, a step in the process, a tissue used to mop up the emotions until Justin realizes that he really wants the girl he had before.

But this time, the girl he had before wants him back, too.

"Anyway," Sylvia says with a laugh, oblivious to my inner meltdown. "Sorry to talk your ear off. It's just nice to see a familiar face. I don't know anyone on this side of town. We should get together sometime. Jus said you were the one who taught him how to crochet. I've been dying to learn, but every time I ask him to teach me he ends up using the yarn to tie me to the headboard."

She laughs again and something in my forehead swells, bigger and bigger, until my head starts to pound and my vision begins to swim.

"But if you have time to teach me, I can pay you back with brunch and Bloody Mary's or something. I make a killer Bloody Mary."

"I have to go," I mumble, patting the counter near the sink blindly for a moment before I realize that I left my purse on my chair in the restaurant. "Sorry, I just remembered I have an appointment."

"Oh, okay," Sylvia says. "All right. Nice talking to you, Libby. See you around."

"See you," I echo as I head for the door on numb legs. I stumble through the increasingly crowded restaurant, going more and more numb, until I feel like a zombie, something alien and only half human shambling through the throngs of happy people.

Had I seriously imagined that Justin might want to be with me? Had I actually thought that what we'd started was something special, and that I would be able to make this work because I know Jus in a way no other woman ever has? Because I know about his inner goofball and his secret, tender heart and that most of the time when he fails at something it isn't because he doesn't have what it takes to succeed, but because he lets his fear of letting people down get the better of him.

He hates to let people down. He wants to make everyone happy all the time.

And maybe that's all this was between us. The sweet words and passionate kisses and the way Justin swore that I made him as crazy in bed as he made me were all part of not letting down a friend who desperately needed his help. Maybe all this time, he's secretly been feeling sorry for me, pitying poor Libby, the socially inept virgin who needs step-by-step instructions to give a blow job, and making plans to go back to Sylvia as soon as possible.

Sylvia, who no doubt learned about sex and love the old-fashioned way, not by googling articles on average penis size, and who has never once doubted that her vagina is a stunning enchanted seashell destined to delight the men lucky enough to kneel before her and swear fealty to her love tulip.

Love tulip? God, Libby, what are you twelve?

"Sorry, I have to run, guys," I squeak out back at the table, fumbling sixty dollars from my purse and placing it near my water glass, hoping that will cover my part of the check since it's all I have in my wallet and I can't fathom the idea of staying here a second longer. "I've got volunteer work early in the morning."

"Libby volunteers at the animal shelter near the school," Bethany informs Roger, clearly still doing her best to smooth the path for romance. "She's always making the rest of us normal humans look lazy."

"What do you do there?" Roger asks, his dark eyes lighting up. "I love dogs. I've got three, and every time I see a stray I'm tempted to bring home another."

"I mostly socialize the cats," I say, hooking my purse over my shoulder.

Because one day I'll die alone and leave only my cats behind to mourn me. But it could be so much worse. At least my destiny is cuddly and furry.

Simple pleasures—tea, cats, yarn.

There is nothing wrong with simple pleasures.

But sometimes you want pleasures that aren't simple. Sometimes you want to be kissed like you're the only woman in the world, touched like you're irreplaceable, and made love to with a passion that makes it clear you are the answer to every question, the balm for every wound, the dream that will still be beautiful and true when all the other dreams have gone yellow and faded with time.

"See you all on Monday." I wave at the table at large, blow Bethany a kiss because she really is so sweet and thoughtful, even if her efforts to help me on the path to true love are coming a little too late.

If only this happy hour had happened a week ago. But it probably wouldn't have mattered. Sooner or later I would have realized that Roger wasn't the man for me.

As I curl up in bed, in the sheets that still smell a little like Justin, I can't imagine loving, or making love, to anyone but him. I can't imagine feeling beautiful and free, unashamed and sexy, powerful and perfect with another man, which means it's time.

It's time to stop fooling myself and do what I should have done a long time ago.

The next morning, I write my landlord a check for the pet deposit, and at the end of my volunteer shift, I come home with a fluffy orange tabby named Ivan the Terrible. Terrible is five years old, blind in one eye, and fat enough to nearly dislocate my shoulder while I'm hauling him upstairs in the carrier. He likes to lick and sniff exposed toes in an affectionate but borderline creepily way that has kept him from being adopted thus far. He's a little weird, like me, and I'm sure we're going to grow old together beautifully.

Or older, anyway. I know the chances that Terrible will be one of the tribe tasked with witnessing my sad and lonely end are slim. He's no spring kitten, so odds are we'll only have ten or twelve years together, at most.

For some reason, the thought makes me cry as I'm setting up his food and water bowl and fluffing up his new cat bed. I cry and cry, until eventually Terrible stops licking my toes through my socks and starts licking my face, purring as he does because apparently my tears are delicious.

"Sicko." I smile as I hug him closer and pet his soft fur. "But I'm glad you're here."

Terrible will be here when it's all over and Justin has been set free to return to his life of dating women who are in his league and I am free to snuggle up with my new cat and be Libby with no romantic complications.

Just the way I like it.

Liar, the inner voice whispers, but it's already quieter than it was last night.

Give me another month or two and maybe I won't remember that I fell in love with the wrong person, or how he made me feel magical, sexy, transcendent things I never imagined I could feel. Maybe I'll be able to forget that for a few days Justin felt like home, and that I never got the chance to tell him how much he means to me.

Though, maybe I should let someone other than my new cat help me forget…

On impulse, I pick up my phone and shoot a quick answer to the text I received this morning while I was knee-deep in semi-feral cats—*Dinner sounds great. Meet you at the Fox Brass at seven.*

I don't have to be at the game, as long as I'm there to talk to Justin after. And it will be easier to talk if I don't have to spend a few hours watching him skate. Because he is really, *really* sexy when he skates. Even before we were more than friends, there were times when watching him on the ice was enough to send a humming, buzzing, *aware* feeling dumping into my bloodstream.

This will be better. I'll have dinner, keep my mind on other things, and then get it over with as quickly and painlessly as possible. I'm going to make it easy for him. It isn't his fault that this went off the rails. He never lied to me or led me on. He was honest from the beginning.

No need to make him feel bad for something I did to myself.

CHAPTER
Twenty—Five

Justin

The seat I reserved for Libby near the bench is empty.

It's empty, which means she's up in a suite somewhere with a bunch of tech billionaires who are probably circling her curvy little body like sharks, picking out which delectable part of her they're going to bite first.

I swear to God, if one of them touches her, I'm going to give Laura that fight she's looking for. We can lock ourselves in her office and scream at each other until she realizes that I'm not the bad guy—she is, for sticking her nosy nose where it isn't wanted or needed.

Libby never asked to get set up with a tech douchebag. Even before she and I started sleeping together, she had a much different romantic future in mind. She wanted a dork named Roger who graduated head of his class at Oregon State, collects rare coins, and is a member of the Antique Book Preservation Society—some of the many things I learned about him yesterday while googling the competition and deciding there is nothing he has that I don't have.

I did okay in college, despite an insane practice schedule, I can develop a love for coins if that's something Libby is into, and I read way more than she gives me credit for.

I read a book last night, in fact. It was a book about how people are completely irrational and do stupid things that they should know better than to do because that's the way our brains are hardwired by instinct and society. It was enlightening in many ways, both in pinpointing the ways in which corporations are taking advantage of my stupidness with evil advertising strategies, and in figuring out why it took me so long to realize that the way I feel for Libby is so much more than friendship. I'd been brainwashed into thinking love had to be a lightning strike, but now I know it can be like taking off a pair of blinders and seeing what was right in front of you all along.

Hopefully she'll still be there by the end of the third period.

If she hasn't been roofied and kidnapped by a tech billionaire.

"What kind of person throws her little sister into a room with twenty single men who have been drinking since the fucking stadium opened?" I pant as Brendan and I tromp down the tunnel toward the locker room, sweaty from an ugly second period in which Brendan took a stick to the face and I got body slammed into the glass by two rookies from the other team. "And don't tell me again that Libby's a grown woman. Yes, she's grown, but she's also used to dealing with elementary school teachers, crafty people, and the hippie dudes she volunteers with. She has no experience fending off douchebag billionaires."

"You could be a billionaire someday," Brendan says. "If you'd get off your ass and talk to my financial advisor. You're not investing the way you should be."

"I don't want to be a fucking billionaire." I rip off my helmet as we hit the rubber floor and stomp into the locker room. "I just want to fucking talk to Libby so I can quit losing my fucking mind."

"Language." Brendan nods to the couches near the television in the corner, where a tiny red ponytail is just visible over the back of the black leather recliner. "Chloe's here. My sitter called in sick last minute. Laura's going to come get her before the end of the game so Chloe's gone before people start showering, but she had some PR stuff to do first."

"Right. Sorry." I sniff hard, holding back all the unflattering things I would like to say about my best friend and her fucking temper and her fucking inability to see that Libby is different. Libby isn't a rebound. Libby is the reason it never worked with anyone else. Chloe loves Laura, almost as much as she loves me, and I'm not ready to give up my place as number one uncle because I badmouthed La in front of her.

"Whatcha making, squirt?" I lean over the back of the chair to see Chloe scribbling madly on a giant pad of paper. The kid is always drawing. She's a coloring demon, who goes through crayons faster than I go through stick tape.

"Seagulls," she says, not looking up from the page. "Very scary seagulls, because seagulls are scary as crap and everyone needs to know about it."

I swallow a laugh as Brendan says in his Dad voice, "Language, Chloe."

"Scary as heck?" Chloe asks, hopefully.

"Just scary is good enough. Your picture will do the swearing for you." Brendan shakes his head at the mass of black and gray wings, interspersed with razor-sharp beaks and the occasional splashes of red, covering his daughter's paper.

"Is that blood?" I ask, unable to repress a snort of amusement when Chloe says—

"Yes. Seagulls like blood with their bread. Human blood."

"They do not," Brendan says, sounding tired. "You got pecked one time, baby, and it didn't bleed. It was an accident. The birds were just excited to be fed."

"Guess you won't be feeding the seagulls again any time soon." I grin at him as he rolls his eyes.

He steps away, running a hand over his sweat-damp hair. "No, we won't. I thought it would be fun, but they ended up mobbing us on the pier this morning, and Chloe got scared. I don't think she would have cried, but she was still a little off after leaving school early yesterday."

"Yeah, about that," I say softly, not wanting Chloe to hear. "I think she faked it somehow, man. She was very perky for someone who was supposed to be running a 102-degree fever. She made me play ten rounds of Exploding Kittens and beat my butt every time, and when I took her temperature at your place it was only 99 degrees."

He sighs heavily. "Yeah. I know. She hates her new school. She wants to go back to the place where she went to kindergarten, but they don't have a good afterschool program or art every day or any money for music or sports or much of anything else. The private school is better. Hopefully she'll see that once she makes new friends and gets settled in."

I'm about to suggest he chat with Libby about why Chloe's having a hard time—who better to give advice than a teacher who loves her kids as much as Libby does—when my phone dings in my locker, and like Pavlov's dog I start to salivate.

I know what those dings are. They're Libby

sexts, flooding into my phone in a naughty stream of wonderful wickedness. I know I should wait until the game is over to read them—we're up by five points, and though I doubt I'll see as much ice time in the third, Coach could always decide to send me out more if things get hairy in the final period—but I can't help myself.

I spin my combination and grab my phone from the top shelf. But instead of Sext Goddess offerings, I see the following from Laura—

I hope you're proud of yourself. Libby bailed on the suite seat and decided to watch the game from a sports bar. Alone, I'm guessing.

So instead of meeting new people, and maybe finding a guy who would be able to see how absolutely amazing she is, she's by herself, waiting for you to get finished playing so she can meet up for a meaningless hookup. And yes, I know all about your "arrangement." She told me yesterday.

But if you think that Libby is the type who can have a no-strings-attached fling and then go back to being friends, you are clearly insane.

She's always had a soft spot for you, and I saw the way she looked at you yesterday. She's falling for you, Justin. Hell, maybe she's already fallen. Maybe it's too late to keep from breaking her sweet heart, and if it is, I swear I will never speak to you again.

Because if you break her heart you're going to break mine, too.

She's not just my sister, she's my best friend. I know her better than anyone, even you. I know that she feels things more deeply than normal people, that she cares so much it's painful sometimes, and that she has always struggled to fit in. But that's not because there's something wrong with her. It's because there's something wrong with a world that expects us to pretend we're not at the mercy of our fears and our feelings and our need for love and acceptance and all the other things that make us vulnerable and human.

But the people who feel big feelings are the best of us.

Libby is one of the best of us.

So make this right, Justin. If you can. Call it off before it's too late, or let her down so easy she feels like she's landing on a bed stuffed with the wooly fluff of baby angel sheep. Even if our friendship means nothing to you, I know Libby does.

Do right by her. Please.

And if you see me after the game, don't try to talk to me. I'm going to be with Chloe, and I refuse to lose my temper in front of her, but I'm not ready to talk to you in person without raising my voice.

I curse as I toss the phone back onto the shelf, then I immediately turn to Brendan and apologize.

"It's okay. I don't think Chloe can hear anything but the echoes of seagull screams right now. What's up?"

I shake my head. I don't know what's up. Libby isn't at the game, she hasn't texted, and Laura is making more sense than I would like for her to.

She's right. I need to make this right. I should

have insisted Libby talk to me yesterday. I should have written her an email, even though the "I don't want to talk until after the game, so leave me alone" message was coming through loud and clear in her last text. Instead, I listened to the voice in my head that swears it's always better to play it cool. The voice that does its best to shut down displays of feelings and fear and other vulnerable human shit that might fuck with my image as the guy who has it all together.

But like it or not, I am vulnerable. If Libby tells me she doesn't want anything from me but my dick, it's going to hurt like hell.

And no amount of playing it cool or fucking other women or crocheting granny squares until my fingers fall off is going to make it better.

I need her. I need her as my friend and as the woman in my bed every night. I need her as the person who makes me laugh, who talks me back from the edge when meditation won't cut it, and who comes to me when she's broken and trusts me to do my damnedest to fix her. I need her for parties at her parents' place and long walks in the woods behind the houses where we grew up together, and because all my best memories have Libby in them.

"I've got to do something." I pace back and forth in front of my locker. "I've got to do something big."

"Don't ask her to marry you," Brendan says. "It's way too soon. You'll scare her."

I spin back to him, emotion galloping through my chest.

Brendan smiles. "Scary, isn't it? When crazy shit like that doesn't seem so crazy anymore."

I nod numbly. It is scary, but a good kind of scary. And the thought of spending the foreseeable future with Libby doesn't make me feel claustrophobic or depressed or trapped the way it did with Sylvia. I would feel damned lucky to spend every Friday night with Libs, whether we were going out or staying in or having a bunch of crafty friends over to make shit together. I want to make things with Libby. Things like love and happiness and afghans and maybe five or six babies so that we'll have lots of small people to share in how good it is to be a family together.

Shockingly, the thought makes my throat tight and my eyes sting a little. "Fuck."

"Seagulls are as scary as that, too," a little voice pops up from behind me. I jump guiltily and turn to see Chloe holding up her finished drawing behind me. "See?"

"I'm sorry Chloe. I shouldn't have said that."

She shrugs her shoulders and wrinkles her freckled nose. "It's okay. I've heard it before. Daddy says it when he drops things on his foot. He drops things a lot when he's making dinner. Even just macaroni and cheese."

"From the mouths of babes," Brendan mutters. "You want me to hang that on my locker, baby? As a public service announcement to anyone thinking about going to feed the seagulls?"

Chloe grins, but before she can answer, my big idea comes crashing to the front of my brain and I kneel down, taking her little hand. "Hey Clo, do you mind if I borrow a few pieces of your paper? And your markers? I promise I'll pay you back."

"You don't have to pay me back," she says sweetly. "I'm really good at sharing. You can have as much paper and markers as you want."

"But you've got like five minutes before we need to head back out," Brendan warns as I hurry across the room, grateful I didn't bother taking off my skates. "Don't you need to meditate?"

"This is better than meditation." The only thing stronger than the mind is the heart. And my heart needs to get a message to Libby's ASAP.

CHAPTER Twenty-Six

Libby

Roger and I are completely compatible.

We like so many of the same things—biking around the city, cats and dogs, keeping arts in schools as much as our shrinking budget allows, craft beers, hiking, skiing, and making brunch last at least two hours on a sunny summer morning. Even the things we don't have in common—needlecrafts for me and antique book preservation for him—are compatible. They are both quietly nerdy and lovely things to be passionate about.

But as far as a mutual passion for passion, we're never going to get around to finding out more about that.

I have absolutely no urge to hold Roger's hand, let alone anything else.

Accepting this dinner invite was a mistake. All

I've done is create a situation that will make things awkward at work when I pass on a second date, while doing absolutely nothing to keep my mind off Justin. Of course, the fact that the Fox Brass has the game playing on the big screen behind the bar isn't helping things.

I should have asked Roger if we could change locations as soon as I realized the pub owner is a Badgers fan, but I'm a glutton for punishment. My eyes keep drifting to the screen, soaking in the sight of Justin playing with his typical mixture of ferocity and grace, while my thoughts drift to all the other physical things he does so well…

"What about the chocolate cake to share?" Roger taps two fingers on the table as he surveys the dessert menu, a gesture I'm realizing is a nervous habit for him. "Or maybe the cobbler?"

"I'm completely stuffed," I say, though I've barely eaten anything. I've been too nervous about my impending talk with Jus to enjoy the meal. My grilled vegetable sandwich tasted like sawdust and the craft brew might as well have been Pabst Blue Ribbon for all the impression it made on my tormented pallet.

"Maybe a coffee, then?" Roger taps the table again. "I'd love to talk more. I know we've worked together for years, but I feel like I'm just getting to know you."

I'm about to tell Roger that I'm just getting to know me in a lot of ways, too, and that I've realized I'm not ready to date someone I work with—*blame it on the job, Collins, that way he won't get his feelings hurt*—when a hubbub from the bar draws my attention. A girl in a Badger's jersey squeals in excitement, the men surrounding her laugh, and a group of older men at the other end of the bar grumble amongst themselves, apparently not approving of the excitement of the younger crowd.

Or maybe they don't approve of what has excited them…

"Oh my God," I murmur, sitting up straighter in my chair as I see what's happening on the screen.

There, sitting on the far end of the Badger's bench as the third period gets ready to start, is Justin, holding a brightly colored piece of paper up to the glass.

A poem for Libby:

My fingers drift to cover my mouth as he switches the sign out for another. His intense gaze is focused on the camera filming him, and I swear it feels like he's looking straight at me as he flips slowly through the stack of papers in his lap.

Dear Libs, I suck at art.

And my first poem to you was a joke about farts.

But this is real and true

Don't call this off. 'Cause I'm stupid in love with you.

In love with me…

He's in love with me! And I'm in love with him! And I've been stressing out for the past day and a half for no reason.

Oh yeah? What about Sylvia?

"Sylvia doesn't matter," I murmur. "Sylvia must be confused."

"Excuse me?"

I turn back to Roger with a start. God, this man used to make me so nervous, and now for a moment I'd completely forgotten he was sitting next to me. "I'm so sorry, Roger, but I have to go."

His lips curve in a wry smile. "Because you're Libby." He motions toward the screen. "His Libby."

I nod. "Yes. Yes, I am." I am Justin's, and he is mine, and I need to be where he is immediately, even if I'll have to wait for him to get off the ice to tell him that I love him, too.

I pull my wallet from my purse, but Roger stops me with a hand in the air. "No, this is my treat. Thanks for coming out tonight. I had a nice time. I hope we can be better friends from here on out."

"Of course, but are you sure?" I wrinkle my nose. "I don't feel right letting you pay."

"I insist," he says with a smile. "I'm just sorry it took me so long to get up the courage to ask you out. If you and Mr. Super Sexy Famous Hockey Player Guy break up, maybe you can give me a shout out?"

I press my lips together, but Roger saves me with a laugh.

"I'm kidding," he says. "I'm happy to be

friends. And I hope everything works out for you two. Truly. He looks like he's suffering. I'm glad you're going to put him out of his misery."

My breath rushes out. "Me, too. And I know you'll find someone wonderful. You're a really nice person with so many admirable qualities. Don't be afraid next time. Go for it. I'm sure any woman you ask out will be thrilled to say yes."

Roger winces. "Okay, now you're being too nice. Go get your guy before I have to man-cry into what's left of my beer and talk about my last ugly breakup."

I nod, giving him a thumbs-up. "Right. I'm gone. See you Monday. Thank you so much for dinner."

And then I turn and hustle across the bar, past the big screen that is now showing footage of the game in progress. But as I pass I hear one of the commenters say, "Looks like someone's got it bad," and another joke back, "Not as bad as that poem. I think my five-year-old could write something better than that. But hey, whatever works. Hopefully this Libby person will realize he has other admirable qualities. Like one hell of a wrist shot."

"I liked the poem. Loved it, in fact," I mutter as I push out of the bar and set off at a jog down the sidewalk toward the arena. It's a good fifteen blocks, but I can't stand the idea of waiting for a bus or a cab right now. I need to be in motion, on my way to Jus and the future and all the unexpectedly amazing things it will hold.

CHAPTER
Twenty-Seven

Libby

At the arena, I head for the staff entrance, pulling out my phone to text Laura and beg her to come let me in, but when I round the corner my sister is already waiting for me, huddling in her puffy white jacket between two stoic faced security guards.

When she sees me, her breath rushes out and a worried look tightens her usually elegant features. My sister is easily one of the most beautiful people I've ever met, but when she's worried she looks like a mole that crawled out of its hole expecting the dark of night and found morning sun instead.

"Okay, so this is happening, isn't it?" She takes my hand, holding tight as she leads me toward the door. "You just did the romantic comedy heroine dash through the airport to catch the guy you love before he gets on the plane, didn't you?"

"Yes, but it was just the street. And that wouldn't work anymore with airport security and boarding passes and stuff," I say, still panting from my run. "But I do love him, La. I was lying to you yesterday. And myself. At least a little. I'm sorry."

She pulls me inside and shuts the door, closing us into the dimly lit hallway that leads to the staff offices and the locker room beyond. "You don't have to be sorry. You just need to be sure you're ready for this, Libs. You know he has a history. He's sworn he has feelings for the rebound girl before."

"I'm not the rebound girl," I say without a shred of doubt.

Laura's lips curve on one side. "No, you're not. I've never heard him use the 'L' word, let alone write it down and whip it out for show-and-tell on national television. The guy legit has it bad."

"Me, too," I say, a smile stretching wide across my face. "I can't wait to see him."

"Oh, you're going to see him." Laura motions for me to follow her as she bustles down the hall. "But everyone in the stadium needs to see you, too."

"What?"

"You two can't start something like this in front of a stadium full of fans and hundreds of thousands of people watching across the world and then leave them hanging." Laura snorts at the ludicrous idea of privacy. "They deserve to see the happy ending, Libby. What kind of PR manager would I be if I let you get away with giving Justin his answer behind closed doors?"

My feet stop moving for a few seconds, and I end up jogging to catch up with Laura and her much longer legs. "What are you saying? You want me to go out there? On the ice?"

"No! Not on the ice. That's against regulations, and besides, you can't skate worth a shit." She covers her mouth as she pauses in front of her office door and adds in a softer voice, "Hey, no cussing in here, okay? I'm watching Chloe for Brendan. Her babysitter bailed at the last minute, and she obviously can't stay in the locker room while the guys are showering after the game."

"As if I'm the one who needs to be warned to watch my mouth in front of children," I say, scowling as I grab a handful of Laura's coat and hold on tight. "But I still have no idea what you're talking about. I don't want to make a scene, Laura, I just want to—"

"Too late for that, babes." She breezes into her office, where Chloe is stretched out on the furry white rug near Laura's desk, drawing a truly excellent cat with long curvy whiskers that seem to have a life of their own.

Chloe glances up, grinning and kicking her feet when she sees me. "Hi, Libby! Justin is in love with you! He used my markers to make his poem. And it had the word fart in it, and my dad thought that was a terrible mistake, but I thought it was awesome. Didn't you think it was awesome?"

I laugh, even though I'm still extremely wary about whatever evil scheme La is working up. "Yes, I did think it was awesome. That drawing is awesome, too, honey. You are so talented!"

Chloe shrugs. "I am. I might be an artist when I grow up. Or a human rights attorney like my mom used to be. Or a professional skier."

"That sounds amazing. Maybe you can be all three," I say, chest tightening as I turn back to Laura and whisper, "I wish they could stay like this forever. By the time my kindergarten girls reach third or fourth grade the change in their confidence levels is so disheartening. The self-esteem of our girls in this country is a national crisis and I—"

"Yes, I agree," Laura says, patting my shoulder briskly. "And we should have a long talk about that later, but for now let's concentrate on getting you camera ready."

"Camera ready?" I squeak, eyes going wide.

"Your hair looks great, as usual—you're so lucky to have such thick hair. But your nose is a little shiny," Laura adds, moving around her desk. "Let me grab my makeup bag. I know your skin is darker, but I've got this great translucent powder that—"

"Laura, I'm not going on camera. I'm going to text Justin to let him know I'll be waiting for him outside the locker room when—"

Laura pops up from behind her desk, clapping her hands together as her eyes light up. "Not a text! A sign! Like his, but with no farts in it because I agree with Brendan that there is nothing romantic about the F-word."

"Fart isn't the F-word," Chloe helpfully points out. "The F-word is—"

"We know," I say at the same time Laura says, "Don't say it, Chloe, or your dad will kill me. And I don't have time for death right now. I have people who love each other to bring together."

"No, Laura." I cross my arms over my chest and shake my head. "I'm not turning this into some publicity stunt. This is important and private and—"

"It's not a stunt," Laura says, whipping out her powder and dabbing a brush lightly into the lid. "It's an act of celebration and inspiration, a beacon of hope for all of us still swimming in the rough waters of casual dating, getting mauled by sharks."

"Or pecked by seagulls," Chloe says, coming to stand next to Laura as my sister fixes my face against my will.

"Yes, or pecked by seagulls," Laura agrees. "What was your dad thinking, taking you to feed seagulls? They are so freaking scary. They're like sky rats, but bigger and meaner."

"You're telling me," Chloe mutters, eyes narrowing as Laura moves on to the blush. "Makeup is kind of like coloring, isn't it?"

"It is." Laura smiles down at Chloe with affection. "You want to do mine for me sometime?

Chloe grins. "Yes. Definitely. Tomorrow."

Laura laughs. "How about Tuesday? You can ask your dad to bring you to practice and we can hang out."

"This all sounds very nice for the two of you." I hold up a hand as Laura whips out something called a moon glow rod that looks sticky, and I'm pretty sure I don't want on my face. "And while I believe in spreading hope, I don't think—"

"Then you're not thinking hard enough." Laura drops the moon glow rod back in her bag and leans down, holding my gaze with an intensity that makes me blink in surprise. "I've been dating for over a decade, Libby, and I have never had a man look as hopeful and adorably desperate over me as Justin looked holding up that stupid poem for you. Hearts all over the country are breaking for that goofy, handsome fool, and when you go out there with your sign that says you love him, too, you're going to put those hearts back together again. And you're going to give them a reason to believe that maybe their own happily-ever-afters aren't a hopeless cause after all."

I stare into my sister's eyes, seeing the

romantic dreamer hiding behind the PR guru, and sigh. "Okay. But I'm doing this my way."

Chloe takes my hand and nods seriously. "You should always do art your way. And you can use my markers. I have crayons, too, but they can be harder to see."

I grin. "Thank you, wise redhead number two."

Laura claps her hands together. "Wise redhead number one will get you cleared to head up the tunnel as soon as the clock runs out, and then be right back!"

Ten minutes later, I've got my own poem ready to go. It's the quickest thing I've ever written, but it feels right. At moments like these, words don't have to be elaborate or fancy or arranged in groups they've never been arranged in before.

They just need to be true and from the heart.

CHAPTER
Twenty-Eight

Justin

We're up by six, with two minutes left on the clock, but I'm back on the ice again because apparently ripping my heart open and showing all the gooey insides to an entire arena full of people makes me score like nobody's business. All I'm thinking about is Libby and whether or not she saw the poem and whether or not she's happy or pissed or embarrassed or secretly hating me for taking something that should have been between the two of us and making it a big public deal.

I should have fucking considered that before, but all I could think about at the time was reaching Libby before it was too late and she decided to end it via text as soon as I stepped off the ice.

It didn't hit me until the entire arena started

cooing and cheering and clapping that I might have made a slight error in judgment, considering Libby enjoys the spotlight about as much as I enjoy getting my legs waxed—which I did once after losing a bet with Travers my rookie season, back before I realized that Travers seems like a big, cuddly teddy-bear type of guy, but is actually evil, never makes a bet he doesn't know he's going to win, and feeds on the shame of rookies like a blood-sucking vampire.

Travers is a damned fine defender, however, and when he slaps the puck back across the line into goal-scoring territory, I'm right there to catch it and do my best to get that motherpucker into the net.

I may be having a hard time thinking of anything but Libby, but I just scored two goals in the third period, after already scoring one in the first, and now coach wants me out here going for a "hat rack."

A "hat rack" is Coach Swindle's non-thing that he's trying hard to make a thing. But it will never be a thing because what the fuck does that even mean? A hat rack? A hat trick—three goals scored by a single player in a single game, originally coined when a cricket player was rewarded with a hat after hitting three wickets with three consecutive balls—is obscure enough. But at least it has history and tradition and people generally know what the hell you're talking about.

A hat rack could have any number of hooks or

padded pillows or whatever it is you hang hats on. And who, in these modern times, own enough fancy hats to necessitate a hat box, let alone an entire rack?

But I know better than to talk sense to people who have their hearts set on naming things that don't need to be named, and scoring another goal might keep my mind off Libby for another fifty seconds…

Forty seconds…

Thirty seconds as I dart around Nowicki, who for once is actually paying attention during the tail end of a period, but it doesn't matter. Because he is a normal guy playing hockey, and I am a demon possessed with the need for this game to end so I can find Libby and tell her in person that I need her more than I've ever needed anything. More than I need to hit a scoring goal this season, more than I need that endorsement deal Brendan assures me is going to help me negotiate a bigger salary, more than I need my family to stay healthy and my friends to be happy and the people I care about to believe their dreams can come true.

Fuck, I want to believe dreams can come true.

Twenty seconds…

I cut around the defensemen and circle behind the net, going so fast I'm balanced on the edge of one skate and about to lose purchase on the ice. My blade chatters, but I stay upright long enough to see Nowicki clear and coming in fast. I saucer pass the puck, which does a double bunny hop, and lands right in front of Nowicki, like a finely wrapped box of chocolates.

Ten seconds, and that rookie slaps the shit out of that beautiful present I hand-delivered to his stick, but the goalie is a fat bastard with a stupidly fast right leg. The puck bounces off his toe—off his fucking toe. God the goal is so close I can taste it, salty and tempting in my mouth, and I pounce on the juicy rebound.

Five seconds and the puck is mine, all mine, and I whip that black biscuit right between Big Bastard's legs. It hits the net a split second before the buzzer sounds and the crowd loses its damned mind. Wild, roaring, rabid-Badger-fan victory sounds fill the air like sweet, extremely loud music, and I thrust my stick in the air with a "Hell, yes, Portland!"

Soon I'm surrounded by the rest of my team, who pound my back and knock affectionately on my helmet, while more hats rain down onto the ice all around us, proving that maybe there is something to the hat rack thing, after all.

I don't know, I only know that as I skate back toward the bench to grab a seat and see if I'm going to make one of the three stars of the game—yes, I realize it's pretty likely, but I prefer to keep shit humble until my name's called over the PA—that I only have eyes for the woman on the other side of the rain of Badger ball caps.

A woman in a red coat and a white pompom hat, holding a sign that says:

Roses are red, violets are blue,
Guess what, Cruise?
I love you, too.

A strangled sound rips from my throat—I'm so fucking relieved I literally choke on it a little—and I break from the rest of the team, zipping across the ice like I'm gunning for another goal.

And I am. But it's a different goal, a better goal. It's Libby, *my* Libby with her silky hair falling around her shoulders and her brown eyes glittering just for me and a smile on her face that tells me she's every bit as crazy about me as I am about her.

Around me, I'm dimly aware of the change in the quality of the shouts and cheers coming from the crowd, and I realize we've been spotted. But I don't bother playing it cool or dialing back my happiness to a more respectable level or worry about what kind of show we're putting on for the fans. A few thousand people might be watching, but this moment is all for Libby and me.

I skid to a stop in front of her, snowing on her boots, and reach for the sign.

"I didn't have time to write a better poem," she says softly, letting me take the sheet of paper and toss it onto the rubber floor at her feet.

"What are you talking about, Collins? That's the best fucking poem I've ever read."

She bites her lip. "Yeah?"

"Yeah," I say, slipping my hands around her waist. "As long as it's true."

"The truest thing I've ever felt," she says, her words becoming a yip of surprise as I sweep her into my arms, spinning in a circle on the game-ravaged ice as I kiss her, holding nothing back.

There are skate scars and ruts beneath my feet that make for a bumpy ride, the crowd is cheering so loud that the air around us vibrates like a train is rumbling by inches away, but for me there is only Libby. Libby's lips and her taste and her tongue dancing with mine. Libby's curvy body pressed to my chest and her arms clinging tight to my neck and her heart beating in perfect rhythm with mine.

"I love you, Elisabeth Collins," I mumble against her mouth. "Will you be my girl?"

"I will. On one condition."

"Anything," I say, knowing it's true. I will do anything for this girl, this woman who has taken my black and white world and shot it through with heart-stopping color.

"We keep the same rules. No lies, no holding back…" She pauses, before adding in a softer voice, "And if it ends, we do our best to make it easy on the other people we love."

I gaze into her eyes and jump right into the "no holding back" water, head first. "And what if it never ends, Libs? What if I want to spend the rest of my life being the lucky bastard who gets to come home to you?"

She blinks faster and her lips part. "Well, I…I guess that would be okay, too."

"Okay?" I scowl, and she laughs as she kisses me.

"Better than okay," she murmurs. "So much better than okay that you should take me home right now so I can show you how much better."

I squeeze her tighter. "Give me five minutes. I was so stressed out about losing you that I scored a bunch of goals in the last period and probably need to get back to the bench so they can start calling the three stars of the game."

She arches a brow as I set her back on her feet just inside the tunnel. "Sounds like you don't need a Sext Goddess for good luck after all."

"Oh, yes, I do," I say, as I skate backward. "And I'm going to show you how much as soon as I get you alone, Collins."

I cruise backward toward the bench, eyes locked on a smiling Libby the entire time, while the crowd continues to cheer because the only thing better than a hat rack is a hat rack followed by romance on the ice. And when my name is called as number one star, it's great, but not nearly as great as the moment when I get back to the tunnel and get to kiss Libby some more while my teammates hustle by giving us good-natured shit for being grossly, publicly, disgustingly in love.

But in between the calls to "get a room" and "let her come up for air, Cruise" I hear Chloe calling out to Brendan, "Daddy! Daddy, I did it! Justin and Libby are in love because of my paper and markers and because art is magic!"

"I think it's love that's magic," I whisper against the skin of Libby's neck.

"Agreed. Though your cock's not too shabby, either."

My eyes narrow as I pull back to gaze into her deceptively sweet looking face. Damn, I knew I'd make a dirty talker of her sooner or later, my naughty, delicious little Libs. "And your vagina is an enchanted crevice of wonders untold."

She giggles. "An enchanted crevice?"

"I didn't want to say cave. It's too sweet and tight to be a cave."

"You're so weird." She shakes her head as she reaches up, cupping my scruffy face affectionately in her hands. "Now get dressed as quickly as possible, please, so I can take you home and get you undressed."

"Your wish is my command, beautiful."

And it is. She commands me onto my back on the floor as soon as we walk in my front door, and I have her the first time with her on top, her skirt bunched up around her waist and her sweater and bra pushed up so I can get my mouth on her tits because we're too desperate for each other to take the time to take our clothes all the way off. Afterward, I carry her to my bed and undress her slowly, carefully, doing my best to memorize how stunning she is as she looks up at me with love and lust mixing in her eyes.

I kiss her everywhere, swirling my tongue

around the place where her pulse beats heavy in her throat, down the elegant curve of her clavicle, across her nipples, which are already hot and pulled tight. I make love to her ankle, the hollow behind her knee, and the whisper soft skin of her thighs. And when I finally glide back inside her, thrusting deep into my beautiful girl as we both cry out in relief to finally be as close as we need to be, it's even better than the first time.

It's so right that right isn't a good enough word for it.

But I'm too far gone to think of a word that means right and home and love and safety and adventure all at the same time. All I can do is hold Libby close as she comes on my cock and then let myself get lost—and found—right along with her.

CHAPTER
Twenty-Nine

One Year Later
Justin

Somewhere out there, in the crowd of friends and family dancing, laughing, and roasting marshmallows over beach fires that flame brightly against the bluish pink of the sky darkening above the waves, is the girl I'm going to marry.

As soon as possible.

Tomorrow, if she'll let me whisk her away to the courthouse or Vegas or wherever we can get the deal sealed the fastest.

But knowing Libby, she'll want to wait and plan something beautiful because she loves planning things.

Like my twenty-ninth birthday party, which is by far the best party I've ever had. Bar none. From the location—a guest house on the ocean with enough rooms to house all my best friends and their significant others, in addition to a cavernous basement where the kids attending will roll out their sleeping bags—to the delicious, gourmet comfort food, to the kites and Frisbees and other games Libby brought to play on the beach, it has been a perfect day.

And if I have anything to say about it, it's going to be an even more perfect night.

"You ready?" I ask Nowicki as I swipe my suddenly clammy palms on my jeans and cast a quick glance down the path leading up through the dunes. Libby is going to be here any second.

Nowicki claps a firm hand on my back. "Ready. Anyone who comes looking for you or Libby will be told that you took a long walk on the beach."

"And no one goes up the secret staircase," I remind him, though I know he doesn't need to be reminded. Nowicki has come a long way in the past year. His focus on and off the ice is laser sharp. He won't let me down, and he's the only person I trusted not to let something slip about my top-secret plan. The rest of my friends and family are too close to the issue.

The issue, of course, being me and Libby making it official and setting a date to get started on forever.

"No one up the staircase," Nowicki echoes. "I'm going to head out so I'm gone before she gets here. You've got this, Cruise."

"Thanks, man. I appreciate the help," I say,

swiping my stupid sweaty palms on my jeans again.

I'm ninety-nine percent sure Libby's going to say yes, but that one percent margin of error is apparently enough to give me a raging case of hyperhidrosis. That's the name of the medical condition that makes your hands sweat too much. I know this because Libby used it to beat me at Scrabble a few weeks ago. She is not only beautiful, sexy, generous, funny, and thoughtful, but crazy smart to boot.

I am in no way worthy of her, but she seems to love me to distraction anyway.

When she rounds the corner in the path and our eyes meet across the dunes, her face lights up like she's been given a wonderful surprise. Even though it's just me, the man she arranged to meet here at seven o'clock, the same man she's woken up to every day for the past nine months, since I finally convinced her to move in with me and put me out of my misery. Because being apart from her is misery made bearable only by how good it is to come back home.

"Hello, sexy," she says, sliding her arms around my neck and pressing up on tiptoe for a kiss.

"Hello, beautiful." I kiss her with the words as my hands slide down to palm her ass through the sexy white linen dress she's wearing. It's loose-fitting and ruffled at the bottom, but sheer enough to have ensured I've been sporting a semi all day long. "Are you ready for your surprise?"

"I am, but I still say the birthday boy should be the one getting surprises."

"I'm the birthday man, Collins. And birthday men like to spread the gifts around." I take her hand, leading her toward the entrance to the secret staircase, an old servants' entrance from the 1800s that leads directly to the third floor of the home we rented for the weekend. "Besides, I'm hoping it's something we'll both enjoy."

She squeezes my hand, grinning as we start up the stairs. "Hmmm…something we'll both enjoy. I wonder what it could be? Is it a hand or two of poker to help me practice not being the worst player ever?"

"It's not a hand or two of poker," I say, playing along.

"Not a hand or two of poker," she muses aloud. "Is it one of your mom's fresh strawberry-rhubarb pies for us to share, even though strawberries and rhubarb are out of season?"

"Sadly, no, though I think Mom has one frozen that I can steal for you the next time we're over at their place."

"That would be lovely. But no pie now, so…" She taps her finger thoughtfully against my wrist. "Is it ski tickets for opening weekend at Timberline?"

"No, but I'll get those tomorrow."

She laughs. "You don't have to. I was just teasing."

"I know I don't have to. I enjoy acquiring things that make you happy."

"You make me happy." Libby stops beside me at the top of the final landing, in front of the simple wooden door, looking up at me with a warmth that still makes me feel so fucking lucky to be the man who somehow won her heart. "So, I'm hoping the surprise has something to do with you and me and some alone time with no clothes on before we end up in a room right next door to your parents."

I grin and close my fingers around the doorknob. "It might be something like that." I push the door open, revealing a large, open attic space with exposed rafters and a canopy bed draped in sheer gold curtains. The candles I lit just a few minutes ago flicker in small white dishes all around the bed, making the scene pretty damned romantic if I do say so myself.

"Oh, Jus, it's beautiful," Libby says, her hand drifting to cover her mouth as she steps inside. "Like a fairytale." She turns back to me, a sparkle in her eyes that I recognize so well.

"You have an idea," I say, before she can get the words out.

"I have an idea," she agrees, bouncing lightly on her feet. "I'll be Sleeping Beauty and you can come wake me up with a kiss."

"A kiss anywhere I want?" I ask, working open the buttons on my dress shirt.

"Anywhere you want," she promises in a

naughty voice as she toes off her sandals and gathers her dress, holding it up as she skips across the room and jumps onto the bed with a giggle. "But not my lips," she warns, pointing a finger my way as she lies down on the pillows. "Surprise me, Cruise."

"Oh, I will," I promise as she closes her eyes. I study her as I shrug out of my shirt and reach for the close of my pants, deciding she looks more beautiful than any princess I've ever seen. Kate Middleton has nothing on my Libs.

Please be mine, I think as I climb onto the bed and slowly lift her dress, loving the way her breath catches when I reveal her tiny white panties and the smooth expanse of her stomach. For a moment, I think about kissing her perfect pussy or the delicate hollow of her belly button, but in the end, I decide to go for something I know she won't be expecting.

I push the dress higher, until I can reach back between her shoulders and pop the clasp on her lacy bra. Libby traps her bottom lip between her teeth as I push the bra up, baring her breasts and I whisper, "Sleeping princesses don't bite their lips."

She immediately releases her lip, and her face goes peaceful once more. Libby excels at role-playing, and playing professor to her naughty schoolgirl is one of my favorite things. But tonight I'm not going to draw out the game. I don't want there to be any pretend going on when Libby discovers my surprise.

I come onto my forearms, bracing myself on either side of Libby's ribs as I press a kiss just to the left of the center of her chest, right above her heart. Her breath rushes out as I run my tongue in slow circles over the place where her breast begins to curve, and her fingers thread slowly into my hair.

"A heart kiss," she murmurs. "Excellent move, Prince Charming."

"Thank you, baby." I bring my tongue to her nipple, circling and flicking across the tight flesh until she's shifting restlessly beneath me.

"Clothes off," she says, pulling her bra and dress over her head and tossing them to the floor. "I need you naked." She reaches for the waistband of my boxer briefs, but I gently put her hand away, not quite ready for her to discover what's beneath just yet.

"Patience, beautiful." I cup her breasts, rolling both of her nipples between my fingers at the same time. "There's no need to rush."

"But people will wonder where you are," she says, cheeks flushing as she arches into my touch. "God, that feels so good. Harder, please. Oh, yes. Yes, just like that."

"I love it when you tell me what you want," I say, my cock so hard I can feel the soft threads of my surprise starting to dig into the skin around the base of my shaft.

"I love it when you're inside of me." Libby

reaches for my boxers again. "I've been wet for you all day. It turns out birthday parties make me frisky."

"Then we'll arrange to have one at least once a month. Maybe twice." I sit back on my heels, just out of her reach. Things may be going a little faster than I planned, but I still intend to be the one doing the big reveal. "But before I fuck you, Libby, I want to show you what I've been working on."

"What you've been…" Her words trail off and her brows shoot up as I pull down my boxer briefs, revealing my surprise. A second later, Libby starts to laugh—really, really hard—but this doesn't faze my cock in the least because it is completely prepared for and thrilled by her laughter.

"Oh my God, what is that?" She pushes up onto her elbows to get a better look at my cock decoration. "Is that a bull?"

"It is a bull." I watch Libby's face as she surveys my latest crocheted creation with another giggle, waiting for the moment when she realizes why I chose to make a sock puppet bull to put on my cock.

Yes, I'm crazy, but there is a method to my madness.

"Is this because you want me to take your bull by the horns?" She runs a teasing finger up my shaft, toward the face of the bull. "Or do you…" She trails off again, a soft gasp escaping her lips as she sees what I've used to make the ring through the bull's nose.

"Jesus, Justin." Her wide-eyed gaze jerks up to meet mine. "Is that what I think it is?"

"If you think it's an engagement ring that I stitched into a bull sock puppet that I crocheted for my dick because I wanted to do something special for the woman I want to marry more than I've ever wanted anything, then yes. Yes, it is."

Libby's eyes fill with tears as she reaches both arms toward me. "You lunatic, yes! Oh my God, yes!"

I go into her arms, kissing her hard and deep, so happy I can't keep from smiling. But that doesn't keep me from kissing her some more as I pull the bull from my cock and nudge Libby's thighs apart. I want that ring on her finger, but I need to be inside her first, to feel her tight and wet around me and know that I'm never going to have to say good-bye to any part of her, body or soul.

"Yes," she cries out as I push deep, filling her completely. "Yes, yes, yes."

"My new favorite word." I groan as she grips my ass and pulls me even closer, deeper, digging her nails into my tight muscles. "Damn, Libby, you feel so good."

"It's still better every time," she says, moving with me as I begin to thrust in and out, riding her slow and easy, wanting to make it last. "I love you so much."

"So much," I echo, kissing her sweet lips.

And then I flip us both over and show her how much by making love to her breasts with my mouth, licking and sucking and biting as she grinds on top of me until she's panting and moaning and seconds away from losing control.

"Yes, Libby. Fuck, yes, baby. Come for me," I beg. And when she goes, I grab her beautiful ass and pin her tight to me, nudging her clit with my pubic bone again and again, drawing out her pleasure until my cock is soaked with her juices and she's trembling on top of me, boneless and breathless.

Only then do I roll us back over and fuck her hard, slamming between her soft thighs, taking my gorgeous girl until the pressure hits critical mass and I explode. I come crying out her name, the only name I ever want on my lips when I'm drowning in pleasure, as my cock pulses thick and heavy, milked dry by Libby's slick, tight, utterly enchanting pussy.

Afterward, we have a little trouble finding Ferdinand—the name Libby decides to give the cock puppet—and I start to have a minor heart attack, but we finally locate the bull and the ring shoved deep under the covers at the end of the bed. With a sharp tug, I break the thread tying the ring into the puppet's nose, and slide it onto Libby's finger.

"It's beautiful." She holds it up, wiggling her fingers until the diamond sparkles in the candlelight. "And I will treasure Ferdinand forever and ever. Though we'll definitely have to hide anything that looks like a toy, but has ever been on your cock, from the kids."

"Agreed." I sigh, running my hand lazily up and down her bare thigh as we lie side by side, staring up at the symbol of our decision to make a life and a family together. "So I assume that means you want kids, too? Guess we should have talked about that before I popped the question."

"This is a perfect time to talk about it." Libby captures my hand, threading her fingers through mine. "Yes, I want kids, but I want you most of all. As long as I have you, I'm all good."

I smile. "Me, too. Babies will just be the icing on the Libby cake."

She turns her head on the pillow, returning my grin. "We should probably head back to the party. Tell everyone we're engaged and stuff like that."

"We probably should." I cup her breast in my hand, brushing my thumb over her nipple. "But I have a problem."

She bites her lip. "What's that?"

"Talking about getting you knocked up makes me want to fuck you again. Just to practice, you know," I say as I move on top of her. "Make sure I'm going to know how to do it when the time comes."

"Right, practice," she says with mock seriousness as she cups my balls, rolling them gently, making my already thickening cock swell.

"I mean, practice is important. It makes perfect, I hear."

"You're already perfect." I capture her lips for a kiss. And then one kiss becomes two and three, and then I'm sliding back inside my love, making her come for me again while I think about what a lucky bastard I am to have a lifetime to spend with my best friend.

The End

Keep reading for a free excerpt of
Sexy Motherpucker,
Brendan and Laura's story!

Acknowledgements

First and foremost, thank you to my readers. Every email and post on my Facebook page have meant so much. I can't express how deeply grateful I am for the chance to entertain you.

More big thanks to my Street Team, who I am convinced are the sweetest, funniest, kindest group of people around. You inspire me and keep me going and I'm not sure I'd be one-third as productive without you. Big tackle hugs to all.

More thanks to the Facebook groups who have welcomed me in, to the bloggers who have taken a chance on a newbie, and to everyone who has taken time out of their day to write and post a review.

And of course, many thanks to my husband, who not only loves me well but also supports me in everything I do. I don't know how I got so lucky, man, but I am hanging on tight to you.

Tell Lili your favorite part!

I love reading your thoughts about the books and your review matters. Reviews help readers find new-to-them authors to enjoy. So if you could take a moment to leave a review letting me know your favorite part of the story—nothing fancy required, even a sentence or two would be wonderful—I would be deeply grateful.

About the Author

Lili Valente has slept under the stars in Greece, eaten dinner at midnight with French men who couldn't be trusted to keep their mouths on their food, and walked alone through Munich's red light district after dark and lived to tell the tale.

These days you can find her writing in a tent beside the sea, drinking coconut water and thinking delightfully dirty thoughts.

Lili loves to hear from her readers. You can reach her via email at
lili.valente.romance@gmail.com
or like her page on Facebook
https://www.facebook.com/
AuthorLiliValente

You can also visit her website:
http://www.lilivalente.com/

Also By Lili Valente

Sexy Flirty Dirty Series:
Magnificent Bastard
Spectacular Rascal
Incredible You

The Under His Command Series:
Controlling Her Pleasure
Commanding Her Trust
Claiming Her Heart

The Bought by the Billionaire Series:
Dark Domination
Deep Domination
Desperate Domination
Divine Domination

The Kidnapped by the Billionaire Series:
Dirty Twisted Love
Filthy Wicked Love
Crazy Beautiful Love
One More Shameless Night

The Bedding the Bad Boy Series:
The Bad Boy's Temptation
The Bad Boy's Seduction
The Bad Boy's Redemption

Sexy Motherpucker
A Bad Motherpuckers Novel
Coming in May 2017!

PROLOGUE

Laura
Last summer…

The summer breeze off the Pacific is cool and sweet, the setting sun casts a sleepy orange glow over Cannon Beach, and majestic Haystack Rock rises from the waves a few hundred feet from shore, like a benevolent overlord watching approvingly as families take advantage of the longest day of the year to party long after most of these kids would usually be in bed asleep.

All in all, it's an excellent evening for burning underwear.

"Good-bye silk thong," I say, tossing my favorite, most comfortable thong onto the fire. It catches on one of the unburned driftwood limbs, trembling there as the flames lick upward, as if hoping for a last-minute rescue.

But there will be no rescue. All the underthings must go. I've got the entire contents of my lingerie drawer in the duffle bag slung over my shoulder, and I'm not leaving until every bra, panty, and garter belt has been reduced to ashes.

"Good-bye comfortable cotton briefs." I drop a handful of simple black and white briefs into the heart of the fire, where they begin to smolder immediately. "Good-bye lace boy-shorts. Good-bye push up bra, I knew you well."

A soft rumble of laughter alerts me to the fact I'm not alone.

I spin, eyes narrowed, to see Brendan standing behind me in a white button-up with sleeves rolled to the elbow, khaki shorts, and bare feet, looking ridiculously gorgeous, as usual. The man should come with a warning label—Danger: Do Not Look Directly into These Dreamy Blue Eyes for Too Long or You Will Forget That I am Off-Limits and Also Not Interested in Romance and Also Irritating as Fucking Hell.

Brendan is captain of the Portland Badgers, the NHL team my PR efforts have helped lift from relative obscurity to one of the big names in the league. The fact that they've qualified for the playoffs three out of the past five years probably hasn't hurt, but I'm not afraid to take credit where credit is due. I've grown the Badger youth hockey program, increased season-ticket sales by twenty percent, and started a fantasy camp with a waiting list two-hundred people deep.

I work hard for my team, and I appreciate players who make my job easy by being sweet to reporters, putting their game face on when I'm filming spots to play during the games, and smiling for the camera when I put together a meet and greet to build goodwill within the community.

Brendan is *not* one of those players. Brendan is a cranky, recalcitrant, stand-offish, doesn't-play-well-with-the-press pain in my ass, which makes the big smile on his face even more disconcerting.

Damn, he's nice to look at.

It really is too bad that he's determined to

stay above the dating fray. He would make some lucky woman very happy. And maybe make himself a little easier to live with in the process.

"Sorry to interrupt, but I couldn't help myself." He ambles closer, slipping his hands into his pockets. "I had to come see if you were really burning your bra."

"I am. And my panties." I flick another pair of briefs into the flames.

"Is this a feminist thing?" He comes to stand beside me, sending the smell of freshly washed man and an earthy, foresty cologne drifting to my nose.

He must have already been back to his room at the hotel to shower. I'm still in the bikini and oversize cover-up I've been wearing all day, rocking the casual look for the first annual Badger Beach Bum weekend. I'd planned to head up the hill half an hour ago and get cleaned up for the team cocktail party starting at ten, but after a chat with some teenagers who agreed to let me take over maintenance of their beach fire, I decided it was better to burn the underwear first.

The sooner I can put the Panty-gate disaster behind me, the better.

"No, it's not a feminist thing." I wait for the briefs to catch before I add more fuel to the fire. "It's a walked in and caught my boyfriend wearing my underwear kind of thing."

Brendan's brows lift sharply. "Oh. Wow."

"Yeah. I forgot my beach bag this morning. When I ran back to get it I found Henry standing in the middle of my bedroom wearing my lace thong, silk stockings, and push up bra. There was also makeup involved, but that wasn't mine." I toss another bra, proud of how much better my aim is getting. "He's a winter, not a spring."

"I'm guessing this wasn't something you knew about Henry going in to the relationship."

"No, it wasn't. Henry is a seemingly straight-laced investment banker whose hobbies include making money, drinking scotch, playing fantasy football, power lifting, and going on long, aggressively competitive bike rides with other investment bankers. He never made any mention of a love for cross-dressing."

"And if he had?" Brendan asks, picking up a slim piece of wood from the sand.

I shake my head. "I don't know. To be honest, it would probably have still been a deal breaker, but if he'd been up front about it—and bought his own lingerie instead of tainting mine—it would have at least been up for discussion."

"Wouldn't washing everything work just as well?"

"No, Brendan, washing everything won't work." The next few bras hit the fire with considerably more force. "Some taints go too deep for soap. Some taints must be cleansed by fire."

"Like taints that come from being close to your ex's taint," he says, summoning an unexpected laugh from my chest.

"Yes, like that." I peek at him from the corner of my eye. "I'm not used to you being funny."

"It's something I try to avoid as much as possible," he says pleasantly. "It confuses people. Makes them think I'm not going to be a pain in their ass the next time they ask me to spend my Sunday morning eating pancakes with strangers."

"So you saw the email…" I glance up at him, my throat tightening for reasons I can't explain.

He nods. "I did."

"There are worse things than being asked to eat pancakes, Brendan."

"Pancakes with strangers," he corrects, catching the thong that has escaped the flames thus far on the end of his stick. "I don't like strangers."

"Even strangers who are also your biggest fans?" I watch him lower the panties into the fire, my cheeks flushing for reasons I also can't explain.

"Even strangers who are fans. When I'm not away for a game, Sundays are for family." The thong slides onto the coals, and Brendan turns to me, an all too familiar, all too stubborn expression firming his features. "You can courtesy-copy Coach Swindle and the team manager on requests all you want, but I won't be bullied by any of you. Chloe's back from her grandparents' house on Tuesday, so I won't be eating pancakes with anyone next Sunday, or any Sunday in the foreseeable future."

"You can bring Chloe if you want," I say, naively hoping this might be an easy fix. "I would be happy to watch her while you network."

He crosses his arms at his chest. "No."

I take a deep breath, in and out, fighting a wave of irritation. "Come on, Brendan. You know Chloe and I get along like macaroni and cheese. We could eat pancakes together at the kids' table and then color until you're ready to go. It will be fun."

"No."

"No? Just…no?" My volume rises as I drop my nearly empty duffle onto the sand and spread my fingers wide in the air in front of the most frustrating man in the universe. "That's it? No, Laura, I will not allow you to do your job. No, Laura, you will never have my cooperation without a fight. No, Laura, I refuse to compromise no matter how far you bend over backward to make things easy for me."

"That's not—"

"No, Laura," I push on, unable to stop the flood now that I've started, "you are a thorn in my side and I hate you like I hate fans who bang on the glass, so you might as well give up now and resign because you are the worst part of my day. Every day. Bar none."

His gaze softens, and the stubborn jut fades from his jawline. "I don't hate you. Not even a little bit."

I swallow hard, shocked to find my eyes beginning to sting. "Yeah, well sometimes it feels like it. I'm just trying to do my job, you know."

"And I'm just a single dad trying to be there for my daughter."

I nod, the stinging sensation getting even worse. "I know that. And I respect it so much, I really do. I adore Chloe and would never want to take quality time with her dad away from her, but can't we find a middle ground?"

Brendan's blue eyes wrinkle at the edges.

"Are you crying?"

"No." I sniff hard, fighting to hold back the tears insisting it's time to come parachuting out of my tear ducts. "I never cry."

"That doesn't sound healthy."

My bottom lip trembles. "It's fine. I don't need to cry. It's a waste of time. What does it matter if half the people I work with think I'm annoying and useless? I know I do good things for this team."

"No one thinks you're annoying or useless."

"Yes, they do." I sniff again as Brendan's face begins to shimmer from the stupid tears filling my stupid eyes. "But it's fine. Who cares? And who cares if I have to burn all my underwear because I'm not sure what Henry wore when I was gone? And who cares if the first guy I've given a key to my apartment in years didn't trust me enough to be honest with me, and I'm clearly a crappy judge of character who will probably end up married to a serial killer? It's fine, I'm just—"

"Stop it." Brendan cups my face in his hands, drawing me closer. His touch is gentle but assured, commanding, and very…interesting in ways I've never been interested in Brendan before.

I suck in a breath and hold it, blinking fast. Brendan has only ever been my friend, and there are times when things between us aren't even really that friendly. But his face is suddenly very close to mine, and his eyes are burning with an intensity that is confusing, and when he speaks in a soft, husky voice my pulse begins to beat faster.

"I'm sorry I make things hard on you. I'll try to do better."

My forehead furrows. "You will?"

"I will, and I'm going to prove it. Turn around and close your eyes."

My brows shoot up, but before I can ask why I need to turn around, Brendan says, "Do it, Collins. You can trust me."

It's true. If there's anyone I can trust, it's Brendan. He isn't the easiest person to get along with at times, but he is honorable to the core. He is trustworthy and good and, even in the midst of his most stubborn moments, kind.

With a nod, I turn to face the beach and the

ocean. The crowd has thinned considerably in the last half hour. Now there are only a few couples still lounging on their blankets at the far end of the beach, and a trio of horseback riders trot toward the trail that leads up to the cliffs overlooking the water and the hotel parking lot beyond.

"Okay, you can turn around," Brendan says after a moment.

I turn, a confused smile curving across my lips as I see what he's holding in one hand. "Are those boxers?"

"They are." He nods solemnly.

My smile widens. "How did you get them off without taking off your shorts?"

"I didn't." He winks as he steps closer to the flames. "I used to be an Olympic-level streaker back in high school, Collins. I can get in and out of a pair of shorts in two seconds flat."

"Impressive." I nod, refusing to be flustered by that wink. "But I'm not sure I understand the point of this removal of underwear, Daniels."

"I removed them because I'm going to burn

them. In a show of solidarity, and to help remove the taint of any bad feeling between us. Give us a fresh start."

"Oh," I whisper, surprised by how nice a fresh start sounds.

But then, that's what this is really about. I'm not burning my bras because Henry might have worn them. I'm burning them because I don't want to be the woman who was too proud to admit that things with her too-perfect-to-be-true boyfriend haven't been perfect for a while. That they have, in fact, been pretty shitty.

I want a fresh start, to head back into the dating rat race with my eyes open and a commitment to being honest with the men I meet. But even more importantly, I want to burn away the bullshit and make a commitment to being honest with myself.

"You ready for this?" Brendan twirls his boxers in a circle.

I nod, reaching for the last handful of panties in my bag. "Ready."

"On the count of three," he says, holding my gaze. "One, two…"

On three we both drop our drawers into the bonfire. For a moment, the flames dim, fighting for oxygen, but then surge back even brighter than they were before, illuminating the smile on Brendan's face.

"You should smile more often," I say, nudging him with my elbow.

He nudges me back. "And you should stop wearing makeup."

I snort. "No way. I look like a twelve-year-old without eyelashes. Or eyebrows. Or lips, unless I have a sunburn."

"No you don't," he says softly, "you look beautiful."

I shift my gaze slowly to my right and find him watching me with that intensity in his eyes again, making it clear he isn't kidding. "Well…thank you. You're not too bad to look at, either."

He smiles as he shifts closer. "No? Not too bad?"

I shrug. "Nah. I mean, I don't throw up in my mouth when I see you coming down the tunnel all sweaty and gross anymore."

He laughs, his eyes doing this amazing

sparkling thing that is completely mesmerizing, holding me in thrall as he brushes my hair over my shoulder. "Well, that's good. I don't like tripping a woman's gag reflex."

"Right." I blush hard, pulling a Libby—my little sister excels at turning bright red every time anyone mentions anything remotely sexual—because I'm thinking about other ways a man could trip a woman's gag reflex.

Yes, I'm thinking about Brendan's cock and my mouth and all the fun they could have together. Sue me! I have a dirty mind; I can't help it. And the fact that I know he's free-balling beneath those khakis certainly isn't helping things.

Brendan clears his throat with a soft laugh. "I didn't mean it like that."

"Likely story."

"I didn't," he says, still standing way closer to me than he ever has before, sending "gorgeous male in close proximity" alerts tickling across my skin. "I swear. I've been out of the game way too long to be that quick with innuendo. I just meant that I enjoy not making you physically ill."

I nod, torn between the urge to step back—hopefully clearing my head—or to lean in, bracing my hands on Brendan's chest. Touching him is starting to seem like a good idea, a really good idea, though I know for a fact it's not. We work together, we fight as often as we laugh, his life is very complicated, and my last breakup is so fresh I'm still sporting road rash.

But damn, he's sexy and he smells incredible, and the way he's looking at me makes my lungs feel too small and my heart feel too large and my fingertips itch to be buried in his softly curled, dirty blond hair.

"What are you thinking, Collins?" The husky note in his voice strikes a hard blow to my already weakening resolve.

"I was thinking about your quick change," I confess, as he tips his head closer to mine. "What if I'd turned around too soon?"

"Then I guess you would have gotten an eye full," he says, his arm wrapping slowly around my waist. "But better bare than wearing your underwear, right?"

"Yes." My pulse spikes as my breasts flatten against his chest and my body celebrates how incredibly good it feels to be close to this man. I tip my head back, bringing my lips mere inches from Brendan's as I whisper, "I like that you're proceeding cautiously. Giving me plenty of time to come to my senses."

His nose brushes against mine, and his breath is warm on my lips as he asks, "Are you going to come to your senses?"

"I don't think so. That doesn't sound very interesting."

"And what does sound interesting?" His arm tightens around me. "Maybe something like this?"

Before I can respond, his mouth is on mine, and a relieved, elated, dizzily wonderful *wow* feeling rolls through me with a sharp snap. The snap is like a light flicked on in a dark room, a horn blaring on a silent street, the sudden rush of adrenaline when you start to step off the curb and a car you didn't see coming rushes past the second before your foot leaves the concrete.

The snap shouts "Pay attention! Pay close

fucking attention! Something unexpected and potentially dangerous is happening!"

And it is.

Cranky, pain-in-my-butt Brendan is kissing me, and it is the most incredible kiss of my entire life. The sweetest, sexiest, most intense kiss, one that turns my bones to jelly and sets off an electrical storm in my nervous system. His tongue strokes against mine, hungry and demanding, asking for what he needs, and I can't help but wrap my arms around his neck and give it to him.

30679181R00182

Printed in Great Britain
by Amazon